William C. R. Agunwa was born in Enugu, former capital of eastern Nigeria (Biafra) won an open scholarship to the prestigious Government College Umuahia and a scholarship to the University of Glasgow Medical School. He qualified with class prize in surgery followed by house job with the regius professors of surgery and medicine trained at the Royal National Orthopaedic Hospital (RNOH) at Stanmore and Great Portland Street. He became a senior fellow of the Royal College of Surgeons of England and a senior fellow of the royal society of medicine.

He worked as a consultant surgeon in teaching hospitals in England and Scotland and overseas in the Middle East as a consultant surgeon at King Khalid Military City Hospital, Jeddah, King Abdul-Aziz Air Force Military Hospital, Dhahran and the tertiary referral Riyadh Military Teaching Hospital. He also worked as chief of surgery at King Fahad Specialist Hospital in Medina.

He has travelled widely across Western Europe including the Balkans and the Nordic countries as well as trips to USA, Northern Ireland and some Middle East countries.

He started writing before his medical undergraduate days with minor publication in college and parish magazines.

To Gudrun, Nicola and Jonathan.

William C. R. Agunwa

A SHADOWED DAWN

AUSTIN MACAULEY PUBLISHERS™
LONDON • CAMBRIDGE • NEW YORK • SHARJAH

Copyright © William C. R. Agunwa 2021

The right of William C. R. Agunwa to be identified as author of this work has been asserted by the author in accordance with section 77 and 78 of the Copyright, Designs and Patents Act 1988.

All rights reserved. No part of this publication may be reproduced, stored in a retrieval system, or transmitted in any form or by any means, electronic, mechanical, photocopying, recording, or otherwise, without the prior permission of the publishers.

Any person who commits any unauthorised act in relation to this publication may be liable to criminal prosecution and civil claims for damages.

This is a work of fiction. Names, characters, businesses, places, events, locales, and incidents are either the products of the author's imagination or used in a fictitious manner. Any resemblance to actual persons, living or dead, or actual events is purely coincidental.

A CIP catalogue record for this title is available from the British Library.

ISBN 9781528983013 (Paperback)
ISBN 9781398418752 (ePub e-book)

www.austinmacauley.com

First Published 2021
Austin Macauley Publishers Ltd®
1 Canada Square
Canary Wharf
London
E14 5AA

1

'Well, catch me if you can. Damn it!'

The Biafran war was over. But Peter, along with some other Biafrans who had fled the final assault on the Ibo heartland, had sworn to have nothing to do with the new Nigeria. Peter set out to make a new life for himself in a remote village between the Cameroons and the original western frontier of Biafra.

There was a price on Peter's head. He had managed to elude the paid informers. The Nigerians employed them freely to keep tabs on not only wanted Biafrans who had gone underground but also for the most part the general population.

'And they will not catch me alive!' Peter kept swearing to himself as he travelled in many disguises, making his way to the frontier. A priest one day, then a farmer in rags the next, or even a palm-wine tapper. He occasionally sported a false beard and moustache but always kept his loaded Biafran pistol on him as well as some cyanide capsules. He also took with him a sturdy compass and a couple of his army ordnance maps. He hitched a ride very occasionally and with great caution, but mostly he walked and walked. As he got near the frontier he stopped walking. He wiped his face with a bunched handkerchief and read:

STAR BEER FOR STRENGTH – COME IN

Under that sign slumped a larger-than-usual hut which gave the appearance of being supported by some five or six Africans who leaned against it for shade. Their heads were tucked under the eaves of the overhanging brooms of roof thatch.

Ropes of hanging beads were strung over the doorway. Peter pushed through them and, after ordering a beer, fanned himself ineffectually with his hanky. The bar was dark. When Peter's eyes grew accustomed to the deep gloom he saw a row of the locals staring at him. Peter smiled at them. They nodded back dark hellos. Strangely, there was a picture of General Okekwu in the bar. He was the now exiled head of state of the Biafra he was fleeing. Peter could have joined the general when he took off from Uli Airport just before the final collapse but decided otherwise.

The bar floor gave off a ripe stable-smell and was spread with looping rosaries of black ants. Almost immediately, some ants located Peter's feet. They swarmed into his worn out sandals. He stamped his feet and cursed, gasping for breath, with trickles of sweat running down the sides of his face, meeting at his chin and dripping onto his smudged shirt front. A drop of sweat made its way like an insect down his breastbone to nest in his navel.

The temperature was in the upper eighties, but there was no sun: it had risen and, once off the ground, disappeared into shapeless grey haze. A dull sky made the day throb with sunless heat, a kind of cookery worse than sunshine. The steamy air was a sickness; there was no fan in the bar, no electricity.

A dusty bottle of Star lager beer was brought and opened, so warm it spewed suds. The bartender slipped a straw into the bottle.

'A glass please,' Peter asked. 'No deh want straw?'

Straws were favoured here, especially for drinking beer. 'No, thanks,' said Peter.

Straws gave him gas. The bartender lifted out the straw and poured Peter a glass of beer.

Peter tipped his glass and drank. He enjoyed drinking now and again; he liked the bitter sting of warm beer on his tongue, the small bubbles needling his gullet, the taste of pickled nuts, a wash of foam, and so on to yeasty fullness. It gave pleasure.

'How far to Gonzo?' He smacked his lips.

The dozing bartender stirred. 'Gonzo. Not very far.'

'How many miles?'

'No know.' The bartender shrugged. 'You going that side?'

Peter made no reply.

2

Peter was the only son of Chief Ezekiel Ofondu, a wealthy stockfish and palm oil merchant from Owerri who had his trading business in Port Harcourt. Ezekiel had been a sergeant education instructor with the all-embracing British western African army called the Royal West Africa Frontier Force (RWAFF). This force included the armies of Nigeria, Gold Coast (now Ghana) Sierra Leone and the Gambia.

Ezekiel married his home-village sweetheart, Ruth, who at that time was the youngest trained primary school teacher in the local schools run by the Church Missionary Society (CMS).

After four years of desperately trying to have a child, Ruth eventually became pregnant; she had almost given up all hope and had told Ezekiel one night after they had made love with great passion and eagerness on her birthday that she would not object if he should decide to take a second wife. But Ezekiel would hear none of it and chided, 'Stop that foolish talk, Ruth.' And not long after this, with morning sickness and other symptoms she knew she was with child.

The nearer her time drew the more enchanted and devoted a husband Ezekiel became. It made a new bond of flesh between them, a constant reminder of their ever-growing union. When from a distance he watched her indolent gait, her body turning limply on her broadening hips, when he feasted his eyes on her as she lounged wearily in her easy chair opposite him, his happiness overflowed and he uttered between tears and laughter all manner of playful endearments that came to his head. He was over- joyed at the idea of fathering Ruth's baby.

Nothing was lacking now. He felt he had been through the whole of human experience: serenely he settled down with both elbows firmly planted upon the table of life.

After her first feeling of relief and astonishment, Ruth was eager to have the child and so find out what it really felt like to be a mother of Ezekiel's child. She wanted a son. He would be strong as a rock, and she would call him Peter.

When her labour contractions started, and despite her repressed forebodings, Ruth was aglow with hope and expectation as she was driven in their newly acquired Morris Minor car to the maternity clinic. But Ruth's labour was very protracted. The pains came quite regularly, then slackened off. When they started to fall off she was dis- appointed and ashamed. They had gone to the maternity clinic at about two o'clock in the morning. At noon Ruth was still in the delivery room. The pains had slackened again.

She looked very tired and worn now but she tried hard to remain cheerful.

'Do you think I'll ever have this baby?' she asked.

'Yes, of course you will,' the motherly and large-bosomed midwife reassured her.

'I try as hard as I can. I push down but it goes away…' It was well after four o'clock in the afternoon when her labour began to progress. Ruth's voice had shrunk to a whisper and then disappeared as she began to lose consciousness. As the baby eventually came out, the midwife opened the door and motioned with her finger for Ezekiel to come. Ruth looked up when he came to stand by her side. A smile played over her face, an almost unearthly smile, and she clutched feverishly at Ezekiel's arm.

Her hand had started to tremble and gradually released its grip of him as she breathed her last. He knew she was gone. But still he held her. Her face wore an expression of serenity. When Ezekiel saw how still Ruth lay, he threw himself upon her crying bitterly. He was helped out of the room.

'Try to be calm. She has not left you empty-handed. You have a lusty baby boy.' The midwife tried to lighten his dark despair, assuage his pain.

3

Though Ezekiel married again later and had three daughters by his second wife, Ruth's child, christened Peter as she had wished, remained very special to him and he vowed to give him everything his money could buy, especially the best education available. Ruth would have liked that.

When Ezekiel left the RWAFF he set up a lucrative business in Port Harcourt, importing stockfish and selling palm oil and palm kernels. As well as his shrewd business acumen he seemed to have luck on his side in the opportune timing of his deals and transactions. He very soon became a wealthy trader and merchant. His business expanded phenomenally and he established warehouses in Onitsha and Aba. His wealth did not seem to go to his head for he gave generously, and the townsfolk conferred a chieftaincy title on him for his munificent donations to the town's development projects.

Peter had a private tutor as well as going to the local school. He was an intelligent outgoing boy with a winsome smile. He also seemed to have inherited his mother's good looks. Just after his eleventh birthday, he was invited for interview at Umuahia, to the prestigious Government College, having done very well in the common entrance examinations to the government colleges.

When the day came for him to go for the interview, he boarded a steam-engine train at the Port Harcourt railway station, seen off by his father, Ezekiel. It was a brilliant, cool Wednesday and, when he got out of bed early that morning, he had opened the window of his room looking on to the backyard and was watching the clouds, dreaming about the future about to unfold.

The clouds were massing in the west, their black convolutions rapidly rolling nearer while long shafts of sunlight struck around their edges like golden arrows on a hanging trophy; the rest of the sky was clear and white as porcelain.

A gust of wind bowed the young mango and guava trees in the backyard. All at once the rain came, pattering down on the green leaves. After the sun shone again, hens clucked, birds shook their wings in the wet shrubs, and puddles of water running over the gravel carried off a scattering of mango and guava leaves.

'How far away I'll be from here by this time tomorrow,' Peter thought mistily.

For the journey Peter had been given extra pocket money and also took with him a large loaf of unsalted bread, two tins of sardines, a few hard-boiled eggs, some guavas, mangoes, oranges, and two sticks of *suya* – four to six pieces of savoury charcoal-roasted diced beef with nutty crumbs, kebabbed on a sharp-pointed stick.

The Port Harcourt-Kano steam-engine train made up at Port Harcourt was already overcrowded except for the sole first-class compartment usually reserved for high government or railway officials.

'Get off there, you bastards!' The rough-tongued guard was chasing off passengers trying to get on to the roof of the train as there was hardly any standing room in the main train compartments.

Ezekiel had earlier on paid a railway porter to keep a seat reserved for Peter on the train. The porter was on the platform looking for Peter who followed him into the train crowding past people and along the aisle and in through a door to where someone sat in the corner of a full compartment, keeping a seat warm for Peter. He shook the young boy's hand and then left.

The train pulled away very slowly from the station. Peter waved emotionally to his father. He sat back and watched the countryside begin to roll by. There was a big stream which ran noiselessly, swift, cool to the eye. Tall slender grasses leaned above it in a mass, bent by the force of the current; weeds streamed out in the limpid water like green wigs tossed away. Now and then some fine-legged insect alighted on the tip of a reed or crawled over a plant leaf. The sunshine darted its rays through the little blue bubbles on the wavelets that kept forming and breaking; old, lopped trees gazed at their own grey bark in the water. Beyond, the fields with tall savannah grass looked empty for miles around.

And then, suddenly, as the train approached within 20 miles of Umuahia, the whole sky lowered itself into a thick greyish-black blanket. The air became very close and oppressive. A deluge of blinding rain with severe thunder and lightning followed. Within minutes the train had shuddered to a halt, and luggage was being strewn about in the compartments, with passengers screaming hysterically. The ground around the railway track had subsided and the train was derailed. A work-gang was sent up from the next station and three and a half hours later, the train was back on the rails, and arrived late in the evening at Umuahia railway station.

Peter had missed the college bus sent to take arriving candidates from the Umuahia railway station to Umudike, some five miles away, where the college was situated. He found himself in the company of three other late arrivals. One was from Jos in northern Nigeria, the other from Benin in mid-western Nigeria and the third from Douala in southern Cameroons.

They hired a taxi which took them to Umudike. At the college they were dropped off at the entrance of the main administrative block, built mostly of wood and supported on concrete stilts. It once housed German prisoners of war from the Cameroons. The principal's office at the far end of the block contained models of submarines, intricate wood carvings fashioned by the prisoners, notably large-sized and an impressive copy of the battleship *Bismark.*

'Welcome to Government College Umuahia,' the college captain addressed all the interview candidates gathered in the assembly hall. 'Here are your identity badges. You must wear them throughout your stay here. There is also a folder for each of you containing information about the college and the interview schedules. I am afraid that whilst you are here only the English language may be spoken. Good luck!'

After this, he called in the college prefects who would be looking after the candidates. The prefects then showed the candidates to their appointed dormitories in each of the houses of the college: Nile House, Niger House, Simpson House, Fisher House, and School House.

The following morning, the candidates sat down to a diet of written examination papers, the results of which were ready by the afternoon. Candidates who did not perform well were sent home the following day after having the cost of their trip reimbursed, plus a top-up ex gratia payment. The farther candidates had to travel to get to the college for the interview, and the more difficult their means of getting there, the more profit they eventually made on the interview trip.

For the remaining candidates, who had to score a certain percentage mark in the written examination, there was a preliminary *viva voce.* Next, the candidates' sporting abilities and potentials were assessed as they tried their hands at cricket, football and athletics. Being an able swot did not necessarily guarantee a candidate a place in the college. Excellence in sports and in academic pursuits were equally valued.

Candidates being considered for one of the college full scholarships had further oral examinations, as well as borderline candidates. However, the potential scholars usually knew from the tone of the proceedings that they had at least been offered a place at the college.

4

Peter arrived back at Port Harcourt by train on Saturday, three days after his departure for the interview. The following Thursday a formal letter arrived offering him a place at the college plus a full college scholarship. Enclosed was the college prospectus with an *In unum lucent* logo and a recommended list of things he would need for the new school term starting in the second half of September. Peter's uncle Edozie had farms at Abakaliki and Ogoja some hundreds of miles away. It had been a very long time since Peter last saw his uncle so he decided to pay him a visit before his first term at Government College, Umuahia. His father encouraged him. 'You should get out of the town, Peter, and get closer to nature there on the farm. Will do you a power of good.'

Uncle Edozie came up to visit them and he travelled back with Peter in his sturdy Austin saloon car. By the time they neared his Abakaliki farm, it was late at night. Peter was half asleep and roused himself to look at the farm, and saw the dim shapes of low trees, like great soft birds, flying past; and beyond it a hazy sky that was cracked and seamed with stars. Peter's tiredness relaxed his limbs, quietened his nerves.

The car stopped at last and Peter roused himself. The moon had gone behind a great luminous white cloud, and it was suddenly very dark – miles of darkness under a dimly starlit sky. All around were trees, the squat, flattened trees of the savannah, which seem as if pressure of sun has distorted them, looking now like vague dark presences standing about the small clearing where the car had stopped. There was a small square building whose corrugated roof began to gleam whitely as the moon slowly slid out from behind the cloud and drenched the clearing with brilliance. Peter got out of the car and watched it drive away around the house to the back. He looked around, shivering a little, for a cold breath blew out of the trees and down in the fields beyond them hung a cold white vapour. In the complete silence innumerable little noises rose from the bush, as if the colonies of strange creatures had become still and watchful at their coming and were now going about their business.

Peter glanced around the house; it looked shut and dark and stuffy under the wide streaming moonlight. A border of stones glinted whitely in front of him, and he walked along them, away from the house and towards the trees, seeing them grow large and soft as he approached. Then a strange bird called a wild nocturnal sound, and Peter turned and ran back, suddenly terrified, as if a hostile breath from the trees had blown upon him from another world.

As his shoes stumbled over the uneven ground and regained balance, there was a stir and a cackle of fowls that had been waked by the lights of the car, and the homely sound comforted Peter. He stopped before the house and put out his hand to touch the leaves of a plant standing in a tin on the wall of the veranda. His fingers were fragrant with the dry scent of the plant which he couldn't identify.

A square of light appeared in the blank wall of the house and he saw Uncle Edozie's tall shape stooping inside, hazed by the candle he held in front of him. Peter went up the steps to the door and stood waiting. Uncle Edozie had vanished again, leaving the candle on the table. In the dim yellow light, the room seemed tiny, tiny and very low; the roof was the corrugated iron Peter had seen from outside; there was a strong musty smell, almost animal-like. Uncle Edozie came back holding an old cocoa tin flattened at the rim to form a funnel and climbed on the chair under the hanging lamp to fill it.

The paraffin dripped greasily down and pattered on the floor, and the strong smell sickened Peter. The light flared up, flickered wildly, then settled into a low yellow flame. Now Peter could see the skin of an animal on the floor, some kind of wild cat. He sat down, bewildered by the strangeness of it all. Uncle Edozie brought another lighted lamp and showed Peter to his room after giving him a mug of Ovaltine plus some groundnuts and biscuits.

Peter watched the wildly flickering flame of the dying lamp leap over walls and roof and the glittering windowpanes and fell asleep thinking about the stories he had heard about his uncle.

5

When Peter was very little he heard that his uncle Edozie had been a bright lad at school but was self-willed and flew into a destructive rage at the least provocation. There were high hopes for him when he entered secondary school and was consistently top of his class. But then he decided to pick a fight with one of his teachers who accused him of paying amorous attention to his newly acquired wife.

The problem seemed to be that for some reason women found him attractive, despite the off-hand and physically violent manner in which he appeared to treat them. He had punched the teacher in the mouth, knocked him briefly unconscious, and decided to leave the school that night rather than suffer the indignity of being publicly disciplined and expelled. He was last heard of working in the tin mines in the Jos plateau area where he earned very good money and where his drive and organising abilities very soon made him foreman. There he met and lived with a beautiful Fulani woman who, despite the cultural and ethnic differences between them, was very devoted to him. They soon had a baby boy but he found the pressures from his prospective in-laws increasingly intolerable. He upped and left, moving down to Abakaliki, then to Ogoja, to farm with the money he had made in the tin mines.

His crops were cassava, maize and yams. The rains that first year were good; they were coming nicely just as the crops needed them. The farm was about a thousand acres on the ridges that rose up towards a mild escarpment, dry windswept country, but during the wet season steamy, with the heat rising in wet soft waves off miles of green foliage. Beautiful it was, with the sky blue and brilliant halls of air, and the bright green folds and hollows of country beneath, and the escarpment and uplands lying sharp and bare. The sky and the strong sunshine would make one's eyes ache, if unaccustomed.

His second year on the farm was a disaster. One day he was coming up the bush track to his homestead for his midday break when he gazed over the uplands and saw a streak of rust-coloured air. Locusts. There they came. He had read that they attacked in cycles and about the havoc they caused to crops, especially if one allowed them to settle on a farm.

At once he shouted to one of his farm hands who then yelled at the others to start collecting tin cans or any old bits of metal. The farm was ringing with the clamour of these as the farm hands shouted excitedly. Then the smoke of fires rose from all around the farmlands. Piles of wood and grass were then prepared. They were throwing wet leaves on to the fires now, to make it smoke acrid and black. Now there was a long low cloud advancing, rust-colour still, swelling forward and out as Uncle Edozie looked. The air was darkening. A strange darkness, for the sun was blazing – it was like the darkness of a bush fire when the air gets thick with smoke. The sunlight comes down distorted, a thick hot orange. Oppressive it was too, with the heaviness of a storm. The locusts were coming thick and fast. Now half the sky was darkened. Behind the reddish veils in front, which were the advance guards of the swarm, moved the main swarm in a dense black cloud reaching almost to the sun.

'I'm finished, finished,' Uncle Edozie groaned. 'Those bastards seem hell-bent and determined to eat every leaf and blade off the farm in half an hour! And it is only early afternoon… if we can make enough smoke, make enough noise till the sun goes down, they'll probably settle somewhere else, and perhaps…'

Now, on the tin roof of his kitchen, he could hear the thuds and bangs of falling locusts, or a scratching slither as one skidded down. From down on the farm came the beating and banging and clanging of a hundred petrol tins and bits of metal. By now, the locusts were falling like a hail on the roof of the kitchen. It sounded like a heavy storm. He looked out and saw the air dark with a criss-cross of the infernal insects. Overhead the air was thick, locusts everywhere. As he urged his farm hands on the locusts were flopping against him, and he brushed them off, heavy red-brown creatures, looking at him with their beady old-men's eyes while they clung with hard serrated legs. He held his breath with disgust and ran through into the house. There it was even more like being in a heavy storm. The iron roof was reverberating, and the clamour of iron from the farm was like thunder.

Looking out the window, all the trees were queer and still, clotted with insects, their boughs weighed to the ground. The earth seemed to be moving, locusts crawling everywhere; he could not see the farm at all, so thick was the swarm. Towards the uplands it was like looking into driving rain – even as he watched, the sun was blotted out with a fresh onrush of them. It was a half night, a perverted blackness.

Then came a sharp crack from the bush – a branch had snapped off. Then another. And another. A tree down the slope leaned over and settled heavily to the ground. The locusts were pouring across overhead for about three hours. Then came one of the farm hands, Ignatius, crunching locusts underfoot with every step, locusts clinging all over him, cursing and swearing, banging with an old hat at the air. At the doorway he stopped briefly, hastily pulling at the clinging insects and throwing them off, then he lunged into the locust-free living-room.

Ignatius was Uncle Edozie's trusted overseer. They had both worked in Jos at the tin mines, but Ignatius, who was a fellow eastern Nigerian, felt homesick when Uncle Edozie decided to quit, and offered to work for Uncle Edozie on his proposed farming venture.

'All the crops deh finish. Na nothing left,' Ignatius moaned. But the gongs were still beating, the men still shouting. It seemed as if the main swarm wasn't settling.

They were heavy with eggs.

'I think they are looking for a place to settle and lay,' Uncle Edozie speculated. 'If we can stop the main body settling on our farm, that's everything. If they get a chance to lay their eggs we are going to have everything flat with hoppers later on.'

He picked a stray locust off his singlet and split it down with his thumbnail. It was clotted inside with eggs. 'Imagine that multiplied by millions!' he shuddered.

Outside, now the light on the earth was a pale thin yellow, crowded with moving shadow; the clouds of moving insects thickened and lightened like driving rain. Uncle Edozie added, 'They've got the wind behind them; that's something.' Ignatius went back into the battle, out into the pelting storm of insects, wading through glistening brown waves of locusts.

Six o'clock. The sun would soon set. Then the swarm would settle. But it was still as thick overhead as ever. The trees were ragged mounds of glistening brown. The rustling of the locust armies was like a big forest in the storm, their settling on the roof was like the beating of tropical rain. The ground was invisible in a sleek brown surging tide – it was like being drowned in locusts, submerged by a loathsome brown flood. It seemed as if the roof might sink in under the weight of them, as if the door might give in under their pressure, and the rooms fill with them. And it was getting so dark... Uncle Edozie looked up, propped his chin on his right hand and sighed heavily.

Soon afterwards, the air was thinner, gaps of blue showed in the dark moving clouds. The blue spaces were cold and thin; the sun must be setting. Through the fog of insects, he saws figures approach. First Ignatius, marching bravely along, drawn and haggard with weariness. Behind him some of the other farmhands. All were crawling over with insects. The sound of the gongs had stopped. One could hear nothing but the ceaseless rustle of myriad wings. Ignatius slapped off the insects and came in.

'I dey think the main swarm done pass,' he said, still looking harassed. 'Na big, big, *wahallah* this!'

For although the evening air was no longer black and thick but a clear blue, with a pattern of insects darting this way and that across it, everything else – trees, buildings, bushes, earth – was gone under the moving brown masses. Uncle Edozie thought, 'If it doesn't rain in the night and keep them here – if it doesn't rain and weigh them down with water, they'll be off in the morning at sunrise. We are bound to have some hoppers. But not the main swarm; that's something.'

In the night it was quiet, no sound of the settled armies outside, except sometimes a branch snapping, or a tree crashing down. Uncle Edozie slept like the dead, exhausted with the afternoon's fight.

In the morning he woke to yellow sunshine across the bed, clear sunshine, with an occasional blotch of shadow moving over it. He went to the window. Ignatius was already out and about. There he stood outside, gazing down over the bush. Uncle Edozie gazed, astounded – and entranced, much against his will. For it looked as if every tree, every branch, all the earth, were lit with pale flames. The locusts were fanning their wings to free them of the night dews. There was a shimmer of red-tinged gold light everywhere.

Overhead the sky was blue, blue and clear. 'Well, I may be ruined and done for,' Uncle Edozie reflected, 'but not everyone has seen an army of locusts fanning their wings at dawn like this.'

Over the slopes, in the distance, a faint red smear showed in the sky, thickened and spread. 'There they go!' exclaimed Uncle Edozie with some relief. 'There goes the main army, off south.'

And now from the trees, from the earth all around them, the locusts were taking wing. They were like small aircraft, manoeuvring for the take-off, trying their wings to see if they were dry enough. Off they went. A reddish-brown steam was rising off the miles of bush, off the farms, the earth. Again, the sunlight darkened. And as the clotted branches lifted, the weight on them lightened, there was nothing but the black spines of branches on the trees. No green left, nothing. All morning he watched as the brown crust thinned and broke and dissolved, flying up to mass with the main army, now a brownish-red smear in the southern sky. The farms which had been filmed with green, the new tender maize, cassava and yam plants, were stark and bare. All the trees stripped. A devastated landscape.

No green, no green anywhere.

By midday, the reddish cloud had gone. Only an occasional locust flopped down. On the ground were the corpses and the wounded. The farm hands were sweeping these up with twig brooms and collecting them in tins and wicker baskets. Sun-dried or roasted the locusts were a delicacy and tasted rather like smoked fish. They provided food for these farm hands for weeks and weeks.

After their midday meal, Uncle Edozie and the farm hands set about re-planting despite the devastated and mangled countryside and farmlands. With a bit of luck another swarm would not come travelling down just this way. But they hoped and prayed it would rain very soon to sprout some new greenery. It all looked like the aftermath of war. Later that year, Uncle Edozie borrowed some money from the African Continental Bank (ACB) at Enugu and bought another farm in Ogoja where he planted rice, more yams and cassava. This was a huge success, especially as he had invested in a Garri making enterprise using his cassava crops. For sentimental reasons, he never abandoned his Abakaliki farm and this also became very profitable the following season.

Uncle Edozie's private life seemed to Peter to have been shrouded in deep mystery. There were rumours that he had a family at Abakaliki and also at Ogoja, but during Peter's stay at his Abakaliki farm where he mucked in as a farm hand and was given generous pocket-money for his efforts, none of the alleged family came to the house. His uncle kept himself to himself and seemed to look after himself quite adequately.

6

The Sunday before Peter was due to travel to start his first term at Umuahia, a celebration party was organised on his behalf. A school hall was hired. In the early morning, a cow was killed in the backyard of their house by men volunteers. Blood from the slit throat was collected in a big bowl and used for a special dish. The cow was roasted whole over a giant log fire.

Women volunteers started arriving from late morning and set about making different types of *ofe,* or soups, like *okra, ogbono, egusi, okasi* and *onug* or bitter-leaf soups, with either okporoko or stockfish, or with meat. They were also busy making and cooking a variety of beef stews, boiled and fried rice in abundance, fried yam and plantains, *foo-foo,* or pounded yam, fish potage, and assorted puddings. There was thinly concealed rivalry among the women concerning whose dishes people came back to for second helpings.

Festivities got underway by mid-afternoon with a prayer of thanksgiving by the local pastor, followed by traditional dancing alongside the eating and drinking. Gifts of poultry, goats, casks of palm wine – the freshly tapped sweet variety and more mature types which were more potent and favoured by the experienced drinkers – bottles of "Star" lager beer and

Guinness stout galore, paw-paws, plantains, yams, cocoyams, fruit and assorted vegetables, all helped to make the party a jolly affair.

One well-wisher, "Dare-Devil" Jo-Jo, stood up to make a speech, somewhat merry with drink. He looked towards Peter, his eyes focussing with difficulty, and with a belly like a heap of cornmeal. He seemed in a state of cheerful, fuddled good humour. Jo-Jo was a little man with a labile cheeky face and an air of uneasy, if aggressive, jocularity. He was noted for being a witty, some say racy, raconteur. He cleared his throat and began tentatively, 'Young man, I should like to tell you a few facts of life. Um... er... er... you won't learn these from your respectable father...'

He coughed drily. There was dead silence. Peter felt rather intrigued. Some of the womenfolk averted their faces. Just then the hired professional photographer arrived for the customary celebration posed group photographs. Everyone was ushered out into the late afternoon sunshine to the evident relief of the older generation.

Towards the end of the festivities, the local branch of his hometown Youth Welfare Association presented Peter with a Bible and the latest edition of the *Concise Oxfo English Dictionary* Peter said silently to himself, 'Not *another* Bible. If they imagine they are going to make a priest out of me with all these Bibles they have another think coming!'

7

It was a fine Thursday morning. Peter's heart was beating fast with excitement as he boarded the train for his first term at the college. The train was much less crowded this time. He turned around to check that his luggage was stowed away safely and then looked out of the window of the train.

They quickly slipped into a cool and shaded mile or so of the track as a gentle breeze filtered through the waving leaves of a mixed forest of stately palms, lank coconut trees and majestically buttressed *iroko* trees. The trees broke up the erstwhile harsh blinding sheet of sunlight into slanting bars and variegated wedges and trefoils of light that played sportively on the faces of the passengers. A few khaki furred, bush-tailed squirrels darted from one tree branch to another. Soon there was another blaze of sunlight, the thick cruel rays pouring on to the right side of Peter's back and shoulders, numbing and dulling as he felt bruised in these parts which seemed like swollen covering for aching bones. The heat waves beat up out of the rail track, and heat lizards, vivid red and blue and emerald, darted over rocks like flames. Peter's head was almost beginning to swim.

In the far distance, as they followed the long curve of another rail-track bend, thatch-roofed mud huts dotted the grassland, around them chicken runs with scraggy chickens scratching about frenziedly. Bleating goats were resting in the shade of small bushes whose leaves drooped wearily in the sapping hot atmosphere. There were a number of hoe wielding farmers and Peter watched their naked brown backs bend, steady and straighten in rhythmical movement, the ropes of muscle sliding under their dusty skin. Most of them wore pieces of faded stuff as loincloths, some khaki shorts; but nearly all were naked above the waist.

The train arrived punctually at the Umuahia railway station where Peter got off briskly just in time to catch the first college bus trip to Umudike. The next morning, he went through the formalities of registration and enrolment. He settled down quickly to the routines of the college and the first letter he wrote home to his father was full of enthusiasm and his great plans for the future.

Towards the end of his first term at the college, Peter decided to make himself a new catapult. He bound thick rubber thongs to a wooden Y with string, tying the final knot tight and snipping off the loose ends with scissors. He tried a practice shot at a passing bird but missed. The pebble thunked into a nearby sand pit. It was a Saturday afternoon and he was bored with swatting for a class test in Latin expected during the "prep" period on Monday.

Peter walked down the road, wearing a T-shirt, white shorts and Clark's sandals without socks. The early afternoon sun beat down on his head and the heat vibrated from the tarmac. The pale sandy soil bordering the tarmac dazzled up waves of light. He decided to go lizard-shooting with his catapult. The lizards were large, sometimes growing to eighteen inches in length; the females were slightly smaller than the males and were a dirty speckled khaki colour. The males were more resplendent, with brilliant orange-red heads, pale grey bodies and black-barred feet and tails. The lizards looked harmless enough; just basked in the sun doing a curious bobbing press-up motion.

At first, they were ludicrously easy to kill. But the lizards grew wise to the hunters and now scurried off at the merest hint of approach. Some of the lizards clung unconcernedly to the walls like dozing sunbathers unaware of looming thunderclouds. The female lizards rushed into crevices and stayed there as Peter approached. He listlessly picked a red hibiscus bloom off a nearby hedge. Then he dropped the flower on the road and it disintegrated. Peter felt remorse for only a few moments.

Soon he saw another lizard, its red head methodically bobbing, slack torso and long tail motionless, catching the last warmth of the day. Stupid lizard, he thought, sunbathing, head bobbing like that. Peter took his catapult and a pebble from his pocket. He cautiously eased the thick rubber back to full stretch until his rigid left arm began to quiver from the tension. He let go at the lizard. The animal keeled over, its legs twitching crazily like the spinning rear wheel on an upended crashed car. He eased the tension on the catapult and held his breath with the effort, his heart thumping in his ears. He stood for a few seconds letting himself calm down, backed softly away and set off steadily for a nearby bush as sweat began to soak his face and hair. He heard the sound of a car as it negotiated a bumpy rutted track. He soon saw a Ford Transit van lurching along. A man was driving and a woman sat beside him. There was still heat in the afternoon sun and the heat seemed to beat out of the ground. The trees and bushes looked tired from the day's exposure. The leaves of the trees hung limply in the dusty atmosphere. Peter had heard the woman's laugh before he saw the van. He moved off the track and followed the curve of the bend until he saw the van through the leaves. The van was pulled up on the other side of the mud road.

The large sliding door of the van was thrown back and Peter could hear the woman laughing again. The man had his arms around her and his face in her neck. She was saying, 'Please don't, Erasmus, please don't, please, someone might see us.' She was twisting her face and neck away, and half-heartedly trying to push him off.

She wore a blue crepe dress with flower patterns on the hips. There was a deep V in front which showed her breasts swinging loose under the crepe. And the back was cut down to the waist. As the two turned around, he put his hand into the front of her dress and lifted out her right breast. His mouth was on her neck again. She felt her heart beating wildly, and the blood flowing inside her flesh like a river of milk. Her face relaxed and her struggle subsided as her brown full breast lay in his hand. She quickly slipped the crepe dress off her shoulders and let it drop. A few minutes later, she seemed to tug herself free and scrambled around the van into the front seat, her dress crumpled. The man was trying to put on his shirt and zip up his trousers as he joined her in the front of the van.

As their van backed and turned, Peter held his breath in case they should see him. He walked down the track to the college. The lowering sun was striking the nearest house full on and he could feel the heat through the soles of his sandals as he walked back.

8

The following night, Peter had a troubled, restless sleep visited by dreams. He was a little boy again on the tennis courts of the Sports Club where he secretly earned extra pocket money as a ball-boy. The expatriate players, if they liked a ball-boy, as they did Peter, would request his services on their court whenever they played. Peter heard and observed things he was probably not supposed to.

There was George, a Provincial Resident. He was bald and shy and his wife, Bridget, was six inches taller than him. Robin was a civil engineer with Costain's Construction Company, and a bachelor. George told Robin at a cocktail party in the Hotel Presidential of his desire to leave his post and become a writer. Also, wanted kids, two or three, nothing quite like family life. But Bridget had said Africa was no place for children, very risky in so many ways these days. *No place for you either*, Robin thought as he looked at the man's little eyes and his frail earnest features.

A week later, Bridget went to a dance party on her own at the Sports Club, where she met Robin. She had a few gins and tonics and smiled radiantly at Robin, who had drunk a lot more than he was used to. He danced with Bridget and they became friendly more by force of circumstance and chance propinquity than by anything else. At midnight, with no sign of George, Robin offered to run Bridget home. 'Not just yet, Robin,' Bridget said languidly, 'the night is still young. Let's dance a bit longer, and perhaps...'

It was the way she said it and the eye she gave him that suddenly made Robin throb with excitement and lust. As if to test the waters, Robin nuzzled her neck and, with his right hand, gently pressed her relaxed and ample buttocks towards his pelvis. Bridget moaned delightedly and in turn brushed her hardening nipples against his half-bare chest, the upper buttons of his shirt loosened. Bridget was wearing an elegant midi-red skirt and a thin sparkling white cotton blouse with delicate neck and arm frills and pearly buttons at the front; her top two buttons were also loosened. Underneath she wore an absurd cut-away bra.

Robin felt a sharp pleasurable tingle and his brain seemed to cartwheel crazily in his skull. He began to reflect that it possibly wouldn't be such a bad day after all. He'd had problems at work and one of their building labourers had fallen off a scaffolding and was dead on arrival at the Port Harcourt General Hospital. The other labourers had downed tools in sympathy. They wanted the safety of the scaffoldings investigated.

'Every cloud has its silver lining,' Robin said comfortingly to himself. 'I only came here to drown my sorrow and forget that goddamn accident, and see what I am getting in return? What the hell. That's life. The rough with the smooth, eh? She's smooth, alright,' he again confided to himself, as he touched her very intimately from the front of her left thigh upwards. All his earlier pre-conceptions about women and love began to blur. He somehow started to feel a respect for that primitive gulf between men and women, the uniqueness of the sexes, their tongue-and-groove opposites, which provides love with its natural adhesive, and which is a psychic need, like sleep and darkness, and the deepest store of emotional nourishment. All told, perhaps enforced blurring of sexual identities was counter-productive, the male and the female not knowing the best of their natures, being compelled to inhabit some neutral no-sex land in which each is in effect a displaced person. We mortals are indeed dehydrated and ordinary until the oil of love plumps us up, dilates the eyes, puts a glow on the skin, and lifts us free from the weight of time, and helps us see in some other that particular kind of beauty is the crown of our narcissism. Yes, our image of love is the spell we put on others – or fancy we do at least – in order to compel them to enter that particular part of ourselves which egoism has hollowed out to receive them.

An hour later, they got into Robin's Volkswagen van and drove up a track off the main road leading to the Sports Club. Heavy rain beat down remorselessly. To Robin it did not now matter whether it was lust or love that brought them where they were. Love is. And lust is. Either makes all the rules itself, according to the multiple needs of the lover or luster.

Robin slipped his hand in Bridget's as they sat in the front of the van, exchanging through their eyes an all-consuming regard that ignored the rain drumming on the roof and the whole world outside. Bridget curved her lip seductively, and a certain slick fever and strange convulsion of nerves at their physical closeness released all Robin's tensions. A sense of magical freewheeling through a world of new and unimaginable harmonies he never thought existed took hold of him.

However, Robin somehow wasn't quite sure how to take the next step. 'What is it, Robin?' Bridget enquired teasingly. And sensing his mounting embarrassment, helped him by taking his right hand and resting it first on her swelling right breast and then on the left breast.

As they frantically undressed and tried to make themselves comfortable in the back of the van, spacious with the seats folded down, they felt an almighty bang as the side of the van was rammed by a car that had spun off the track where they had parked. Robin was killed instantly, and the driver of the car seriously injured.

The driver of the car was George, Bridget's husband.

9

At the end of his first term, Peter already felt like a grownup as he returned home for the Christmas holidays. He became more interested in those that lived near them like Papa Boyle who lived next door with his daughter, Emily. Papa Boyle came originally from Freetown, Sierra Leone, before settling in Nigeria. He had worked for ten years in Lagos, then moved to Port Harcourt where he retired some years ago as an Assistant Chief Clerk in the Ministry of Lands and Agriculture. His exact age no one seemed very sure about, probably in his seventies, or possibly early eighties.

It was a bright Sunday afternoon in December. Above Papa Boyle's head was his dovecote, a tall wire-netted shelf on stilts, full of strutting, preening birds. The sunlight broke on their grey breasts into small rainbows. His ears were lulled by their crooning, his hands stretched up towards his favourite, a homing pigeon, a young, plump-bodied bird which stood still when it saw him and cocked a shrewd bright eye.

'Pretty, pretty, pretty,' he said, as he grasped the bird and drew it down, feeling the cold coral claws tighten around his finger. Content, he rested the bird lightly on his chest, and leaned against a tree gazing out beyond the dovecote into the landscape of a late December afternoon with trees stretched wide to a tall horizon where some mist lay over the land, swirling away between the trees, or tearing asunder and drifting up into nothingness. Clumps of *iroko* and palm trees stood out here and there like giant black rock. Over the smooth green turf between the trees a dim brown light played in the warm air. Red brown, like tobacco dust, the earth deadened the sound of any approaching footfalls.

His eyes travelled homeward along the green turf between the trees until he saw Rosa, his granddaughter who lived with them, hanging about a wooden shed.

His mood shifted. He deliberately held out his wrist for the bird to take flight and caught it again at the moment it spread its wings. He felt the plump shape strive and strain under his fingers; and in a sudden excess of troubled spite, shut the bird into a small box and fastened the bolt.

'Now, you stay there,' he muttered and turned his back on the shelf of birds. He moved warily along a hedge, stalking his granddaughter, who was now about to enter the shed, singing as she looped over a nearby makeshift gate, her head loose on her arms. The light happy sound mingled with the crooning of the birds and his anger mounted.

'Hey!' he shouted; saw her jump, look back, and abandon the gate.

Her eyes veiled themselves and she said in a pert neutral voice, 'Hullo, Grandad.' Obediently she moved towards him, after a lingering backward glance.

'Waiting for Patrick, I bet!' he said, his fingers curling into his palm.

'Any objection?' she asked lightly, refusing to look at him. He confronted her, his eyes narrowed, shoulders hunched, tight in a hard knot of pain which included the preening birds, the sunlight, the flowers, herself.

He said, 'Think you're old enough to go courting, hey?'

The girl tossed her head at the old-fashioned phrase and sulked. 'Oh, Grandad!'

'Raring to leave home, hey? Think you can go running around the fields any time of day or night?'

Her smile made him see her as he had every evening of that month, swinging hand in hand along the path away from the house with that rough-looking son of a goldsmith. Misery went to his head and he shouted angrily, 'I'll tell your mother!'

'Tell away!' she said, laughing, and went back to the gate. He heard her singing a cheeky love song for him to hear.

'Rubbish,' he shouted. 'Rubbish, impudent little bit of utter rubbish.'

Growling under his breath, he turned towards the dovecote, which was his refuge from the house he shared with his daughter and her husband and their children. But now the house would be empty. Gone all the young girls with their laughter and their teasing. He would be left, uncherished and alone with that square-fronted, calm-eyed, uninspiring woman, his daughter.

He stooped, muttering before the dovecote, resenting the absorbed cooing birds.

From the gate the girl shouted, 'Go and tell! Go on, what are you waiting for?'

Obstinately he made his way to the house, darting pathetic backward glances of appeal at her. Her defiant but anxious young body stung him into love and repentance. He stopped.

'But I never meant...' he muttered, waiting for her to turn and run to him. 'I didn't mean...'

She did not turn. She had forgotten him. Along the path came her young man, Patrick, with something in his hand. A present for her? The old man stiffened as he watched the gate swing back and the couple embrace before they swept into the wooden shed.

Papa Boyle stumped into the house, hearing the wooden floor creak under his feet. His daughter, Emily, was sewing in the living room, threading a needle held to the light.

He stopped again, looking back at the wooden shed. The couple were now sauntering among the bushes, laughing. As he watched he saw the girl escape from Patrick with a sudden mischievous movement and run off through the green turf with him in pursuit. He heard shouts, laughter, a scream, silence. Then more laughter and a longer silence.

'But it was never like that at all,' he muttered miserably. 'It never was like that, why can't they see? Running and giggling and kissing. They'll come to something quite different. Nature did not intend sex to be easy. Everything has to be paid for.'

He looked at his daughter with sardonic hatred, hating himself. They were caught and finished, both of them, but the girl was still running free. He wished he could go back to Freetown and die there in peace.

'Can't you *see?*' he demanded of his invisible granddaughter, who was at that moment rolling in the thick green grass with the goldsmith's son. His daughter looked at him and her eyebrows went up in tired forbearance.

'Put your birds to bed?' she asked, humouring him.

'Rosa,' he said urgently. 'Rosemarie...'

'Well, what is it now?'

'She's over there with Patrick.'

'Now you just sit down and have your tea.'

He stumped each foot alternately on the wooden floor and shouted, 'She'll marry him, I'm telling you, she'll be marrying him next!'

Emily rose swiftly, brought him a cup, set him a plate. 'I don't want any tea. I don't want it, I tell you.'

'Now, now,' she crooned. 'What's wrong with it? Why not?'

'She's twenty. Twenty!'

'I was married before twenty, don't you remember, and I never regretted it.'

'More fool you,' he said. 'Then you *should* regret it. Why do you make your girls marry? It's you who do it. What do you do it for? Why?'

'The other two have not done badly. They have two fine husbands. Why not Rosa?'

'She's the last,' he mourned. 'Can't we keep her a bit longer?'

'Come now, Papa. She won't be living very far from here and she'll be here every so often to see you.'

'But it's not the same.' He thought of the other two girls transformed inside a few years from charming petulant spoiled children into serious and often harassed young mothers.

'You never did like it when we married,' Emily said.

'Why not? Every time it's the same. When I got married you made me feel like it was something wrong. And my girls the same. You get them all crying and miserable the way you go on. Leave Rosa alone. She's happy.' She sighed, letting her eyes linger on their small sunlit patch of vegetable garden.

'She'll marry next month. There's no reason to wait.

'You've said they can marry?' he said incredulously.

'Yes, Papa, why not?' she replied coldly, and took up her sewing.

His eyes stung and he went out to the backyard. Wet spread down over his chin and he took out a handkerchief and mopped his whole face. The backyard was empty.

From around a corner came the young couple; but their faces were no longer set against him. On Patrick's wrist balanced a young pigeon, the light gleaming on its breast. 'For me?' said the old man, letting the drops shake off his chin. 'For me?'

'Do you like it?' Rosa grabbed his hand and swung on it. 'It's for you, Grandad. Patrick got it for you from the market.' They hung about him, affectionate, concerned, trying to charm away his wet eyes and his misery. They took his arms one on each side and directed him to the shelf of birds enclosing him, petting him, saying wordlessly that nothing would be changed, nothing could change, and they would come and visit him often. The bird was proof of it, they said, from their lying happy eyes, as they gave it to him.

'There, Grandad, it's yours. It's for you.'

They watched him as he held it on his wrist, stroking its soft, sun-warmed back, watching the wings lift and balance. 'You must shut it up for a bit,' said Rosa intimately, 'until it knows this is home.'

'Teach your grandmother, bless her soul, to suck eggs?' growled the old man with a twinkle in his eyes.

Released by his half-intentional anger, the couple fell back, laughing.

'We're glad you like it.'

They moved off, now serious and full of purpose, to the gate, where they hung, backs to him, talking quietly. More than anything their grown-up seriousness shut him out, making him alone; also, it quietened him, took the sting out of their tumbling like puppies on the grass. They had forgotten him again. Well, so they should, the old man reassured himself, feeling his throat clotted with tears, his lips trembling. He held the new bird to his face, for the caress of its silken feathers. Then he shut it in a box and took out his favourite.

'Now you can go,' he said aloud. He held it poised, ready for flight, while he looked down the backyard towards Rosa and Patrick. Then, clenched in the pain of loss, he lifted the bird on his wrist and watched it soar. A whirr and a spatter of wings and a cloud of birds rose into the evening from the dovecote.

At the gate Rosa and Patrick forgot their talk and watched the birds. From the living room, that woman, his daughter, Emily, stood gazing, her eyes shaded with a hand that still held her sewing. It seemed to the old man that the whole afternoon had stilled to watch his gesture of self-command, that even the leaves of the palm trees had stopped shaking.

Dry-eyed and calm, he let his hands fall to his side and stood erect, staring up into the sky. The cloud of shining silver birds flew up and up, with a shrill cleaving of wings, over the dark belts of trees and the bright floods of grass, until they floated high in the sunlight, like a cloud of dust motes.

They wheeled in a wide circle, tilting their wings so there was a flash after flash of light, and one after another they dropped from the sunshine of the upper sky to shadow, one after another, returned to the shadowed earth over trees and grass and field, returned to the dovecote and the shelter of night. The backyard was all a fluster and a flurry of returning birds. Then silence, and the sky was empty.

The old man turned, slowly, taking his time; he lifted his eyes to smile proudly down the backyard at his granddaughter. She was staring at him. She did not smile. She was wide-eyed, and pale in the cold shadow, and he saw the tears run shivering off her face.

The following morning, Rosa knocked on the door of her grandad's room with a cup of tea and a piece of toast the way he liked ·it. There was no reply. She opened the door gently and then screamed, dropping the tray with the cup of tea and toast. Papa Boyle was dead, but he had a gentle smile on his face.

10

Peter was a soccer fanatic and before returning for his second term at the college his father gave him permission to go to Enugu to see the finals of a soccer match between the Enugu Rangers and a team from Port Harcourt at the Enugu sports stadium. He was to stay at the home of a family friend living in the affluent government reservation area (GRA) of the city.

The shaded streets in this area were lined with flowering trees, their pink and white blossoms perched on the branches like butterflies among leaves. It was such a lovely, lovely day with gusts of perfumed wind in the gay glittering sunshine. There were some old Spanish-style colonial mansion houses enshrouded in bourgeon villas with their large bright, red-coloured bracts. Even the sky looked different, seen from between these buildings that seemed so fresh and clean with their white walls and red roofs. It was not the implacable blue dome that arched over Uncle Edozie's farm; it was a soft flower-blue and Peter felt he could run into the blue substance and float there, forever at ease and peaceful. It was a different world! Peter wished it were his world there and then and for all time.

That afternoon, Peter took a taxi to the sports stadium and tried to get in early to avoid the expected crush at the turnstiles, but to no avail. Queues had been forming all morning, and ticket touts were thriving. Peter's heart lifted when he eventually got past the turnstiles, pushed along by a vocal group of supporters from Port Harcourt. There were barely ten minutes left before the kick-off.

One of these chaps said, 'The prices they charge in hotels in this damn place! It looks like they don't add them up here; they multiply them!'

It soon became clear that members of the group Peter got caught up with came not only to watch the match but, more importantly, to have fun in the Coal City and escape from their families and workaday pressures for a day or two. As their tongues loosened with a few bottles of Guinness stout and "Star" lager beer, a few more witticisms began to tumble out.

Akuzamus began, 'I think money, not music, is the food of love, especially to women. Never known a woman not cheered up by spending; they then become moved to love and romance while the mood lasts.'

'Obed, what do you reckon is the perfect age for marriage?'

'If you're young, I would advise you to wait, and if you're old, it's too late. Things will always conspire to make the perfect age imperfect.'

Donatus chipped in, 'Love and romance are possible only if you don't know the loved one very well. And if you do, the inevitable nagging and carping is like constant dripping that wears the bedrock of the love relationship. Petticoats have a way of ending up around men's necks. It seems to happen in all forms and strata of society.'

Obinna then declared, 'Men offer romance to get sex and women give sex to acquire domination, love, or money and the implied freedom it gives. Sex is conquest; sex is power. A woman's love frees, and it traps; female sexuality is a delicate affair. Women as a rule are unfamiliar with violence. They have not been through the tussles of childhood and youth the same as men. Deep down in their minds and consciousness I expect defloration and rough sexual love nearly always assumes the aspect of a dreaded surgical operation.'

Obed came back, 'Men and women lack definition without each other. Women need men, if only to get out of the company of other women; and vice versa. In general, I think women have a more calming influence than men. Though they think themselves tops in personal relation- ships, I find that men may even enjoy making fools of themselves, but I've yet to see a woman who takes kindly to being poked fun at or being made a fool of. Maybe, in a curious way, it's because women seem to have more images of themselves than men.'

Kalu joined in, 'It takes a woman to know that a man is trying to hide something unpleasant.'

It was Sylvester's turn. 'You can never be too sure where women are concerned. A woman's face is a fairy tale. The inner woman and her outside and perceived personality are often birds of a different feather. What women feel is often different from what they think. I don't know if that helps give womanhood its elusive depth. But watch out for that inert submissiveness that is to many a woman both the penalty and the atonement when they have been up to no good!'

Donatus suggested, 'Women are just as mono erotic or poly erotic as men except that the forces of economics, biology and conditioning modify how they express their eroticism. Desire and sexual pleasure demand an expenditure of vital force in woman as in man; although receptive in nature and through their sexual anatomy, feminine sex hunger isn't less active than men's and appears to be manifested in a nervous and muscular tension. Apathetic and listless women are always sexually cold. The sex drive is our shared chief passion. It brings the physical and the emotional together. Nothing is so equivocal as a touch, but in these things women never touch men accidentally.'

Akuzamus came back with, 'For most women happiness seems to equal good personal relationships. When a woman is in love, it is the eyes which have the most devastating power.'

Donatus re-joined, 'These days men have to catch up with women's feelings of freedom and liberation, but women still want men they can look up to. Another of their delicate psychological dichotomies. And beautiful women – I just think they are like white elephants; best to look at them, not to own them.'

'Be fair, chaps,' Vincent spoke up, 'women have hardly had a fair deal in the past. Men have not had a biological function imposed upon them which puts the interest of the species and race before their personal interests for a considerable period of their life, restricting choice and transcendency. Men have always used their masculinity against women, and still do; why shouldn't women use their femininity?'

'Assertive sexuality in women, even in marriage, I find quite frightening,' Donatus spoke again. 'Insistent feminism merely leads to sexual trench warfare.'

'Who really knows what goes on behind the closed doors of marriage?' Akuzamus asked. 'Women seem to have an extraordinary ability to withdraw from the sexual relationship, to immunise themselves against it, in such a way that their men can be left feeling let down and insulted without having anything tangible to complain of. They seem able maternally to bestow the gift of themselves as if on a humble stranger and remain untouched. They have their way of making their men feel denied, rebuffed and made to appear brutal and foolish with a sense of guilt. There are innumerable marriages, I dare say, where two people, both twisted and wrong in their depths are well matched, making each other miserable in the way they need, in the way the pattern of their lives demands.'

Peter completely forgot about the soccer match, listening to these sagacious men. When he looked at his watch only a few minutes remained before the end of the game. The Enugu Rangers had just scored an equaliser and the supporters of both camps were shouting and banging fervently to urge their team to sink the other side with a last-minute goal. Peter thought he'd better escape through the main gate before the final whistle and avoid the usual end of game mad rush and scramble to leave the stadium.

11

While attending the soccer match, Peter had seen large billboards at the sports stadium proclaiming a revivalist Crusade meeting there the next evening organised by one of Billy Graham's aides. Having heard a lot about the American evangelist Peter said to himself why not give them a listen before going back to Port Harcourt on Monday and make the most of your trip to the capital city.

Busloads and trainloads of people arrived from towns, near and far, for this brand of "spiritual servicing". The stadium was packed out. The main speakers were three American evangelists supported by a Nigerian evangelist and interpreter. Their loudspeaker public address system was in good, if deafening, voice. There was something stagey about it all that intrigued Peter very much. Various religious denominations seemed to be there. At one corner he saw a small group of smartly dressed Salvation Army children and officers.

A middle-aged man nearby said, 'I heard and saw Billy Graham himself preach and harangue a couple of years ago. Why must these Americans commercialise everything – including religion. But give him his due, I suppose one could call him a smooth Hollywood version of John the Baptist.'

'This lot is catching up fast!' someone else said.

An elderly polio victim on crutches commented, 'I think I prefer the non-frills religion of the salvationists over there. Look at their charity work among the common people.'

'You are entitled to your own opinion,' chipped in a trendy teenager in ridiculously high orthopaedic boots, bell-bottom trousers and wearing a very loud multi-coloured skirt. 'These salvationists get on my nerves. They can be as mean as hell if you'll pardon the expression. They're not nearly as generous as they seem. I should know, having been in one of their establishments. Someone once described William Booth, their founder, as a sensual, dishonest, sanctimonious and hypocritical scoundrel... a brazen-faced charlatan... a pious rogue... a tub-thumper... a masquerading hypocrite.'

'How dare you!' shouted the polio victim, angrily. 'Belt up, you empty-headed layabout or I'll clout some sense into you with one of these crutches. '

Many cripples came hoping for miraculous cures. A choir from a church in the Uwani layout suburb of the city supplied the background choral music.

The first speaker mounted the platform gingerly. He was a burly six-footer with keen penetrating eyes and a massive jowl. He was a Baptist from the so-called Bible-Belt of the southern United States. He began, 'I was a wicked sinner before I met Christ. I quit my prosperous business interests to train for the ministry and have never looked back on my decision. My Lord Christ has been more than generous in providing for all my needs.'

With the Bible in his left hand and a lot of gesticulating with his right arm, he continued. 'The five crucial relationships of life are... Man and God... Man and Man...

Man and Nature... Man and Himself... God and Nature... Life is all about relationships. Friendship is the cornerstone of practical Christianity. Christ's life is a comment on friendship. He called His disciples friends... Man's life is worth what God is prepared to pay for it: His Son's life... A genuine disciple is one who discovers the truth, freedom and sonship that are found in Christ. Man must give up both his virtues and vices to find Christ... God's love through Christ, like marriage, responds to need, not worth; it is exclusive. The true Christian's creed is expressed in his conduct; his conduct derives from his creed. Future goals determine present behaviour... Religion without the life of God has no meaning and no power... Cracking the shell of surface religion is the constant goal of faithfully seeking the truth. Once men get their view of God wrong nothing can be seen straight... Only Christ can blend the different tones and tongues of mankind into music... Christ's friendship brings both blessing and responsibility...

'Christians, however in the world, are together one nation... All people matter equally to God, even if there are inequalities in the circumstances of life... The story of the Good Samaritan and *Who is my neighbour?* is that God cares who you show compassion to regardless of deeply felt racial, religious, political, sexual and cultural differences.'

He mopped his forehead, dripping with perspiration, with a large white handkerchief, sat down sipping a glass of water. The choir gave their rendition of the hymn, *Amazing Grace,* as the second evangelist prepared to take the rostrum. Peter couldn't remember much about the features of the second evangelist except for his slightly balding head and large ears. He looked cheerful and self-assured. He began: 'Faith invites us to borrow on God's account, trust in Him and He will repay... Faith should be no mere wishful thinking and credulity; it rests on God's promises, and is rooted in sure historical events and past personal experiences... Faith is immediacy after reflection, and with faith, believing is seeing... Faith is not trying to slit open the nightingale to find the song... A life of resigned faith is surprised by joy and love... Faith is like the mainsail of a boat – useless when packed up in its sail bag, but very potent when stretched out to receive the wind of God's power... Faith is to trust now and understand later. It is entering the frightening world of God: a flight into the absurd and irrational...

'Christ refuses to pander to proof seekers, but gladly responds to those in need... Saving faith is always personal faith... Salvation can never be by proxy... Beyond the moment of the first personal confession, faith often has to stumble on the pathway to further revelation... The glory, the mystery, and the otherness of God's truth are beyond the limited grasp of our finite minds and frequently an offence to a secular outlook...'

He continued. 'Christianity is suffering servanthood, and the way of the Cross is not a spectacle the disciples are asked to observe; it is a route they are expected to follow... You can't stay for ever in the place where God spoke to you; you have to get moving to the place he is promising you. We must never let the past shackle us... Life is an unending circle of experiences...

'Christian life is a way of death, Christ's death, finding freedom in suffering... In Christ, imperfection is part of perfection... The Christian message is that we are all potential gods and goddesses... Only when God is at the centre of our lives do we experience true security... The power of God is worked out in the experience of weakness... True Christian faith is about enabling power... the life of God being born again in the slum of man's heart... True religion affirms the value of the human life from the first breath to the last in the face of an indifferent universe. Christianity is a religion of grace, not merit; salvation is by faith plus nothing.

'A caring God does not wind up the universe like a clock and put it on the mantelpiece and then go away... Suffering is God's alarm clock, God's megaphone to wake a sleeping world... The universe is one of cause and effect... To Christians, life on earth is a one-off experience... Give me life with its struggles and victories, with its failures and hatreds, with its deep moral meaning and its unknown goal: to me that means a life of faith...'

He sat down, still smiling, and reached for his glass of water.

The third evangelist rose to speak. He was small-built, nervous, energetic, with close-springing mousey hair, white freckled skin, quick deep-blue eyes. He looked busy, hard-working, essentially pragmatic, practical and humane. Peter liked him. He began, 'Priorities are crucial to practical Christian living and are the difference between Christianity and Pharisaism. Just rushing around trying to be good and helpful is often a form of escapism. The graveyard is full of indispensable people. We can understand ourselves only in the light of inner events. The world within us and the world about us are intertwined... Living is easy with eyes closed... There is no personal morality outside social terms.

'Each life is an experiment and we will be judged for not being ourselves... Christian discipleship should be progressive because God's revelation is continuous... There is no retirement in the service of God... The Christian life entails new experiences to draw out new resources and potentials from us.

'The greatest gifts are nothing without the determination to use them, and those less well-endowed can do great things with commitment... God's gifts are for daily use – not cold storage... Heaven is not a lump-sum payment for good deeds but where the road goes... Christianity and true religion should bring the touch of eternity into everyday affairs... Man plots, God plans... Christ's death is divine folly... True greatness is only found in service, using the gifts and resources that the Holy Spirit chooses to give us and not constantly moaning for others which he has not given us... Pride is spiritual arthritis; makes us too stiff to stoop and serve.

'Love and arrogance cannot co-exist. Love is to use our freedom to give away our freedom... Love is the best kind of truth we know... It is the same everywhere... Love creates beauty and is proved in consistent action more than in fervent language... God's love has hard edges which can bruise us when we take it for granted.

'The heart is the centre of thinking and attitudes... The soul is the centre of vitality and personness... It is the heart which perceives God... God reveals himself in the vulnerable and broken in heart... Any deep experience is only really valuable when it happens to you.

'The greatest miracle in life is that of individuality, and this only develops in freedom and love... We all have a basic hunger for recognition and status, and making our mark is the driving force of life and living... Praise, like food and drink and love, is a basic necessity of life. We all need to know we matter to someone… Appreciation gives life, lightens tasks, lifts loads, quenches those thirsts that diminish life if unslaked… Lord, make us more generous with our cups of water!'

'Christianity searches for the lost, recovers the straggler, bandages the hurt, strengthens the sick, and leaves the healthy and strong to play… Christians think of Jesus; they practise Paul… There is an almost irresistible temptation to tame and domesticate Christianity by our fixed traditions and narrow dogmas. Moral courage is often claimed by people with rigid minds… Zeal is a commendable quality, not blind fanaticism… Jesus requires total commitment, not fanaticism, from his disciples… Even zeal for Christ can become a negative zeal against others, an aggressive superior thing… A fine charitable line separates genuine conviction from fanatic absolutism… Beware of exploitive evangelism of power-hungry men with wafer-thin spiritual veneer inveigling weak-willed and guilt- burdened women and men.

'Popular ethics is based on what is convenient and what is useful: the *bland leading the… Indulge yourself, it's later than you think…* But there is an ultimate standard which will in the end be upheld… There is in man an inherited, unrelenting finger of guilt and accusation which is embedded within the consciousness… It is like a hidden land-mine within the minds of us all… People often try to get relief from its merciless accusation either in stoical self-acceptance or in religiousness.

'Every crisis is a growth point for the Christian, and everything we do in life is bound to challenge our faith…

Every detour in life can lead to a new highway, and every cross become a means of salvation...'

'Dear friends, let us bathe all our witnessing in prayer and remember that God's work done in God's way will never lack either the men or the means... God Bless You!'

When he sat down, the choir sang more solemn hymns including *Abide with me* as people were invited to come up to the rostrum to affirm publicly their conversion to the new life in Christ. They began to troop up in their scores, either suitably penitent and subdued or high with emotion, chanting alleluias and amens.

12

Peter returned to Port Harcourt the following day, and then to Umuahia for his second term at college.

There was a new principal, Dr Elliot-Jones, a former Oxford don. He had come to take over from Dr Holmes now back at Caius College, Cambridge. The teaching staff was fairly cosmopolitan with teachers at various times from a mix of countries – Scotland, Canada, the United States, England, Eire, Wales, India, Australia, New Zealand, Sierra Leone, Gold Coast (now Ghana), and Nigeria.

Peter was good at sports and later became the college cricket and hockey captain as well as a college prefect. He had also joined the recently formed College Cadet Force. This had been the brain-child of Dr Holmes who had served in Germany as a major in a tank regiment during the Second World War and was later stationed in Dusseldorf with the British Army of Occupation. He was assisted by Dr Wilkinson, the senior chemistry master who had himself taken part in the Normandy landings as a captain in a Scottish infantry regiment and was badly wounded in the left thigh by shrapnel, leaving him with a residual, if well disguised, limp.

In his final year at the college, Peter had been awarded the class prize in physics and mathematics and he went on to obtain a Grade One pass in the Cambridge West African School Certificate (WASC) examinations with six distinctions and two high credits in the eight subjects he sat. Peter had told his father even before the results of the examinations were known that he wanted to be an engineer, wanted to do something that was both practical and intellectual.

His father, Ezekiel, soon made all the necessary arrangements for him to proceed overseas to London and fulfil his declared ambition.

Before he flew off to London, Peter went down to visit his Uncle Edozie at his farm once again. Uncle Edozie had never been ill before, although the farm was in a malarial district and he had lived there some time. Perhaps he had had malaria in his blood for years and never known it or developed some form of immunity to it. He always took quinine, especially during the rainy season. Somewhere on the farm there must be, he said, a tree trunk filled with stagnant water, in a warm enough spot for mosquitoes to breed; or perhaps an old rusting tin in a shady place where the sun could not reach the water to evaporate it. Peter saw him come up from the farm one evening, out of sorts and shivering. He offered his uncle quinine and soluble aspirin, which he took and afterwards fell into bed without eating his supper.

The next morning, angry with himself and refusing to believe he was ill, he was off to work as usual, wearing a heavy jacket as a futile prophylactic against violent shivering fits. At ten in the morning, with the fever sweat pouring down his face and neck and soaking his shirt, he came back home and got between blankets, already half-unconscious.

It was a very sharp attack, and because he was not used to illness, he was querulous and difficult. He lay still, half delirious with fever, in an uncomfortable doze. His temperature had not dropped. He was taking the bout very hard. The sweat poured off him; and then his skin became dry and harsh and burning hot. Every afternoon, the thermometer's slender rod of quicksilver mounted in a trice up the frail glass tube, so Peter had hardly to keep it in his mouth at all; higher every time he looked at it until by six in the evening it stood at 106°F. There it stayed until about midnight while he tossed and muttered and groaned. In the early hours it dropped rapidly to below normal, and he complained he was cold and needed more blankets. But he had all the blankets in the place piled over him. At regular intervals Peter went and fetched him cold drinks.

Still, Uncle Edozie resolutely refused to go to hospital. Peter pushed a cushion to the end of a sofa and lay down. It was a close night, and the air in the room hardly stirred. The dull flame in the hanging lamp burned low, making a little intimate glimmer of light that sent up broken arcs of light into the darkness under the roof, illuminating a slope of corrugated metal and a beam. In the room itself there was only a small yellow circle on the table beneath. Everything else was dark, there were only vague elongated shapes.

Peter listened intently and the tiny night noises from the bush outside sounded suddenly as loud as his own thudding heart. From the trees a few yards away a bird called once, and insects creaked. He heard the movement of branches, as if something heavy were pushing through them, and thought with fear of the low crouching trees all about. He had never become used to the bush, never felt at home in it. He still felt a stirring of alarm when he realised the strangeness of the encircling bush where little animals moved, and unfamiliar birds talked.

Peter lay tense on the sofa, every sense alert, his mind quivering like a small, hunted animal turned to face its pursuers. He listened to the night outside, to his own heart and to the low mutter of Uncle Edozie. He fell asleep. Once he startled awake but the only sound was that of his uncle's faint rhythm of breathing. He drifted off to sleep and this time dreamed immediately.

For some reason, in his dream he was back in Enugu; he was trying to catch a flight to Lagos en route to London but the Fokker Friendship plane due to take them had been diverted to Port Harcourt for a long while and it seemed unlikely another flight would be taking off from Enugu to Lagos for another day or two.

Peter decided to drive to Lagos instead and make his connections from there. The small hours of the morning were the only time it was anything like safe to travel. He wound up the Millikin Hill, a skilfully designed route of blind corners, uncambered Z-bends and savage gradients that annually claimed scores of lives as some of the worst drivers in the world sought to negotiate its bizarre geometry. Then through stretches of road that were crumbling tarmacadam death traps he made his way towards Lagos via Onitsha, the Niger Bridge, Asaba, Benin.

Just outside Benin he encountered a roadblock which consisted of three fifty-gallon oil drums surmounted by planks of wood. Parked to one side was a chubby armoured car, surrounded by at least two dozen soldiers wearing camouflage uniforms and armed with sub-machine guns with sickle-shaped magazines. Peter coolly bluffed his way past the roadblock after talking to the captain in charge of the detachment of soldiers. He didn't bother to enquire the reason for the roadblock. He was just glad to get past it.

He arrived in Lagos in the evening and checked in at a hotel. Later that night, after about an hour's delay because of technical problems and wild tropical storms, their plane took off for Kano en route to London via Rome and Madrid. As they approached Kano International Airport, the plane suddenly began to lose height and was plunging into the fields on the outskirts of the walled city when Peter screamed in his sleep and half-woke, fighting off the weight of sleep on his eyes, filled with the terror of the imminent air crash.

He tried to wake himself from the horror as he struggled in the quicksand of sleep. Then he was awake and sitting up, panting. The room was filled with a thick grey light, and the still burning lamp sent a thin beam to the table. Peter struggled in his mind to separate dream from reality. He sat, weak and shaking, thinking of the air crash, trying to clear away the fog of horror.

He looked across the room and saw the Uncle Edozie was sleeping quietly and looked better. Without disturbing him, he by-passed him to the veranda, where he leant forward against the chilly bricks of the balustrade, breathing in draughts of cool morning air.

It was not sunrise yet. All the sky was clear and colourless, flushed with rosy streaks of light, but there was darkness still among the silent trees where crickets seemed to be endlessly telephoning.

All day, Peter watched his uncle grow better hourly, although he was very weak still and not yet well enough to be irritable. Joy, one of the three wives of a neighbouring farmer, Amobi, who became good friends with Uncle Edozie after he had helped Amobi obtain a bank loan, cooked them nourishing meals and generally tidied up the house as Uncle Edozie regained his strength.

He was back at work in a week.

13

Peter arrived at Heathrow airport on a Saturday morning in October. It was piercingly cold and his dowdy tropical suit did little to protect him from the knifing North Sea winds. For a brief moment, he thought seriously about catching the next plane home. He just couldn't imagine himself surviving such a perishing climate.

However, the sight of Harry Uche, a distant cousin who had come to the airport to welcome him, lifted his spirits. Tm glad you came, Harry,' Peter said, not a little relieved.

'I did consider catching the next plane back home until I saw you. Feels like the land of eternal *harmattan,* but colder and without the dust.'

'I felt like that myself,' Harry sympathised. 'But it soon passes and they do have warmer days, I assure you.'

'Thanks a lot.'

'Don't mention it.'

Peter stayed with Harry for the first week in his somewhat cramped flat in Hendon, north London. It was almost like home from home when Harry cooked Peter *fo-foo* and delicious okra soup with tender beef and stockfish cubes, plus fried plantains and yams.

'Hey, Harry, what can I say? I never expected any of this. How come?' Peter asked with manifest surprise and appreciation.

'Nothing, really,' Harry said casually. 'I manage to get the ingredients fairly readily from a market in Camden Town which sells African foods, often cheaper than at home. I'll take you there in the next day or so.'

Harry did most of his cooking on a kerosine primus stove in the flat, and the smells from the cooking hung about the flat for long periods even after opening wide all the windows of the flat.

Peter made his first acquaintance with the London underground two days after his arrival. He managed to lose his purse with traveller's cheques and a little loose cash on the train but was agreeably surprised to recover it intact at Edgware station where someone had handed it in at the terminus of the Northern Line he got on to. Later that day, he went shopping for warmer clothes, especially for a duffel coat, thick jumpers, and thermal underwear, including two pairs of long johns. He was very grateful to Harry and gave him some of the money he came over with.

Harry had come to England four years earlier to study law but did not seem to be getting anywhere with his studies, though he was often very active in organising student meetings and protests. He had even gone to Moscow and Paris as a student union representative. Peter wondered how he managed to combine his extra-curricular activities with serious studying. He was also very partial to female company. Peter soon became increasingly embarrassed to come into the flat and find Harry in compromising situations with his girlfriends.

One evening, Peter found Harry unusually deep in thought as he got out an old biscuit-tin, in which he was in the habit of storing his letters from women. As he dallied among these letters and also among some snapshots from the same biscuit-tin, he examined the handwriting of the letters and their style, both as varied as their spelling. A word would bring back a face, a gesture, a tone of voice; but sometimes he could recall nothing.

All congregating into his mind at once. These women cramped, diminished one another to a single level of love where all were equal. Taking a handful of letters, he played with them for a few minutes, cascading them from his right hand into his left. He said to himself, 'What a lot of sham!' This summed up his opinion. For his pleasures had so trampled over his heart, like schooldays in a playground, that no green thing grew there, and whatever passed that way, being more frivolous than children, left not so much as its name carved on the wall.

Then, he concentrated on the gay and melancholy snapshot of Patricia. He tried to visualise her, but her features blurred in his memory, as though the living and the face on the snapshot were rubbing together and obliterating each other. Yes, Patricia shored herself up against unhappiness by refusing to get involved with a man. She was business- like in her affairs. There were many men but she seldom lost control and never fell in love. Love would have made life unbearable. Sex for her became a small moment set in days of fun; it was a quick unsatisfying fumble on a bed that provided no relief but was over in a matter of seconds and almost forgotten in a week. She expected nothing from it. She only made love to a man after she had got all she wanted from him and, with one disastrous exception, made this plain beforehand. Her love affairs ended with the act of love, which was how she wanted it. But when her affair with Harry ended it produced violence in her. More than mere bitchery, it was decidedly vicious. She hurled things at him, screaming, crying, smashing things.

'I never get it right, this problem with women. I should either leave them alone altogether or take the risk and get married,' Harry murmured dejectedly under his breath.

14

Peter moved to a YMCA hostel in London in the second week of his arrival after thanking Harry for putting him up for the first week. He wanted to lead a life of his own.

He registered at a London polytechnic college and very quickly obtained top grades in his A-Level physics, mathematics and chemistry examination entries. He was called for interview at Bristol University and was offered a place there to study electronic engineering. It was at the interview that he met James Simpson who was also offered a place to study the same subject at the university. They soon became firm friends. James was a Scot from Aberdeen whose father was a minister of the Church of Scotland at Queen's Cross, Aberdeen. He had been to eastern Nigeria a number of times as a kirk spokesman for their missions in that part of the world and knew Enugu and Port Harcourt very well.

James confided later that, though he could have done his studies at Aberdeen University, he was just as happy at Bristol where he got his first firm offer of a place. James was slightly over six feet tall, handsome, and very extroverted. It was at a students' union party organised by him in the Clifton district of Bristol that Peter met Elizabeth Price whom he later married.

During the summer vacation of their second year at the university, James invited Peter over to their home in the Cults suburb of Aberdeen, and also planned to take him on a brief tour of parts of Scotland. In a strongly patriotic tone James declared, 'Some of the most beautiful landscape in Europe is right over there in bonny Scotland. Nae doubt! Legendary lochs and valleys to enchant you, with rugged mountains and gentler hills of heather, and romantic castles amid the breathtaking expanse of wild country... It is all there on a grand scale, just a short drive or walk from our picturesque towns and famous cities.'

Their first stop was Glasgow which Peter found to be richly endowed with museums and art galleries. They visited the Botanical Gardens and saw an extensive selection of tropical plants and the unique collection of tree ferns in the Kibble Palace. At the Palace Museum there was a fascinating visual record of the life and history of the city. Then to the Queen Elizabeth Forest Park, and from its hill- top trails superb views over Loch Lomond, Helensburgh and the Clyde estuary. Next, the delightful scenery of the Trossachs where, after a bit of climbing and walking, they attacked their packed lunch with relish.

Their next stop was Edinburgh, Glasgow's rival city, with its castle magnificently situated on the rock heights overlooking Sir Walter Scott's monument, the wide Georgian avenues, and Prince's Street with its smart shops. The castle with its museum, historic apartments and the Scottish crown jewels on display Peter found most enchanting. They dropped in at the Museum of Childhood in Edinburgh with its unique collection of toys, dolls, dolls' houses, costumes and nursery furniture. They rounded off their Edinburgh visit by taking a trip to the zoo and then having a glimpse of the partly restored Holyrood Palace; finally, they walked the Pentland Hills south of the city.

They then doubled back to the west coast, to the pleasant seaside town of Irvine, near the broad sands and renowned golf course of Troon. One of James's girlfriends, Moira, lived there. She was a second-year veterinary student at Glasgow University. From there, via Loch Earn, they arrived at Perth, on the River Tay. The countryside near the city was lovely and breathtakingly lovely. Perth, Peter was told, had been the capital of Scotland until 1437, their kings being crowned there in Scone Palace. From Perth they travelled on to Aberdeen and then to Cults.

Peter spent a most pleasant long weekend with James's family. They were enjoying quite exceptionally warm, glowing summer weather. James had a younger sister, Helen, who was soon to go to St Andew's University to read languages. James's mother, Morag, had been a nurse at the Aberdeen City Hospital where she first met James's father, Ian when he was brought in by ambulance. He had broken his ankle playing football.

From Cults, they made a short trip to Stonehaven where Peter sampled their renowned fresh fish dishes. Even their fish and chips tasted scrumptiously different. However, the beach there was too pebbly for Peter's liking. From there they went on a longer journey to the magnificent Royal Deeside and up to the Balmoral estates. Peter was astounded by the number and splendour of the castles in the area. Along the way they were forced to make a few emergency stops to avoid hitting deer crossing the road. The whole countryside, the woods and the castles seemed out of this world in the fading sunlight.

15

The March before they graduated, Peter and James made a trip to Paris as a respite from their intensive preparations for their final examinations. When they got there the trees were still leafless, black, cold; but the fine twigs were swelling towards spring so that, looking upwards, it was with an expectation of the first glimmering greenness. Yet everything was calm, and the sky a calm classic blue.

They saw a man and a woman walking towards their boulevard from a little hotel in a side street. The couple drifted slowly along, and almost at once they turned into a cafe and sank down as if exhausted in the glass-walled space that was thrust forward into the street. The place was empty. People were seeking the midday meal in the restaurants. Not all: that morning crowds had been demonstrating, a procession had just passed, and its straggling end could still be seen. The sounds of violence, shouted slogans and singing no longer absorbed the din of Paris traffic.

A waiter leaned at the door, looking at the moving crowds. He reluctantly took an order for coffee.

The man yawned, the woman responded infectiously, and they laughed with an affectation of guilt, exchanging glances. When the coffee came, it remained untouched. Neither spoke.

After some time, the woman yawned again, and this time the man yawned and looked at her critically, and she looked back.

At the far end of the boulevard, there was a faint agitation, like stirred ants, and Peter heard the man say, 'Nothing changes, everything always the same...'

Outside drifted the lovers, the married couples, the students, the old people. There the stark trees, there the blue quiet sky. In a month the trees would be vivid green, the sun pour down heat, the people would be brown, laughing, bare-limbed.

The next day there was a commotion at the other end of the boulevard. This increased and became a serpentine head and a group, presently a crowd, of people sprung from hidden relaxation, lined the curb stones.

'Ecoute! Regarde!' someone cried with a lot of passion.

Boys sprinted past on bicycles, automobiles jammed with elaborate bedazzled sportsmen slid up the boulevard, high horns tooted to announce the approach of what looked like a bicycle race, and even cooks in undershirts appeared at restaurant doors as around a street corner a procession came into sight. First was a lone cyclist in a red jersey, toiling intent and confident out of the westering sun, passing to the melody of a high chattering cheer. Then three together in a harlequinade of faded colour, legs caked yellow with dust and sweat, faces expressionless, eyes heavy and endlessly tired.

'What the hell is going on?' Peter asked, intrigued.

A troupe of fifty more swarmed after the first bicycle racers, strung over two hundred yards; a few were smiling and self-conscious, a few obviously exhausted, most of them indifferent and weary. A retinue of small boys passed, then a few defiant stragglers.

'Cessez cela! Allez-vous-en!' a youth trying to help himself to some apples at a grocer's in the commotion was being told off.

Peter later gathered that the tumult had in fact been a local practice run for the real Tour de France, not due till the end of June or early July.

Peter and James sampled some of the sights and lights of Paris by metro, on foot, and on *bateaux mouches* – Notre Dame cathedral, the Eiffel Tower, Montmartre, Napoleon's Tomb, the Bois de Boulogne, the Louvre Museum and the Tuileries Gardens, the chaotic Place de la Concorde, Champs Elysees, Arc de Triomphe, the Latin Quarter and the Pantheon.

It was a toss-up between taking an excursion tour to the palace of Versailles or to the palace of Fontainebleau. They decided on the longer trip to Fontainebleau. It was an all-day affair; their first stop was the painters' village of Barbizon. They entered a rather attractive old cottage house where many autographed paintings by up and coming, mostly French, artists were on display and some for sale. The lady of the house, probably in her fifties, and wearing a smart calf-length light-blue dress, proudly showed them where Robert Louis Stevenson, the Scottish writer, often sat when he frequented the house.

Peter bought an autographed painting of the palace and James that of the forest of Fontainebleau depicting a girl that looked uncannily like Moira, entwined in an ardent embrace on the grass with her partner, who was lying on top of her whilst the girl wrapped her legs around his posterior and folded her arms and the essence of herself very closely around him.

The Palace, they were told, was the inspiration of Francois I who built the superb chateau decorated by Italian painters and sculptors. Here Napoleon signed the act of abdication and said goodbye to his old Guard.

When Peter and James arrived at the palace, the wrought iron gates were shut. So, they had coffee and snacks and ice cream on the cobbled stone pavement outside the restaurants close to the front gate of the palace. Half an hour later, the gates swung open and they started their guided tour of the palace. The state apartments were sumptuous, and the balcony views of the gardens enchanting. But where Napoleon signed his act of abdication held Peter's interest the most.

Back in Paris it was time to pack up and go back to Bristol the following day. Peter and James both agreed it had been a worthwhile break.

The Channel crossing back home was rough and they were both horribly sick with the pitching and rolling of the ferry. They had intended to buy some duty-free goods, but surviving the crossing put that beyond their immediate consideration. James locked himself in the lavatory during most of the crossing till just before they arrived at Dover. His legs were like jelly as they disembarked, but his spirits began to revive as soon as they got on dry land. He still retched miserably and was ashen faced as they made their way to Paddington station to catch the train for Bristol.

16

Peter and James graduated with honours. James decided to go back to Aberdeen whilst, after their marriage Peter and Elizabeth Price set up home in Southampton.

After their twin children, Emma and Mark, arrived and were about five years old, Peter felt he ought to go back to Nigeria, at least for a while, but he still kept ownership of their terrace house in Southampton. A recruitment mission from Lagos had interviewed him in London and in 1965 he set out with his family for Nigeria to join the Nigerian army with the rank of captain. He was initially stationed in Lagos where he and his family lived comfortably at Ikoyi. Soon afterwards, he was posted to Kaduna to serve as a military intelligence officer. He quickly set about sorting out the overall military set-up in Nigeria.

Unlike politics, where the people thought they knew their rights and quite often fought for them successfully, the average southern Nigerian had little interest in the army except as officers. It was therefore easy for a few interested persons to do whatever they wanted with the army without being challenged, and the British government, being among the interested, had taken full advantage of the situation. For a start, they saw to it that almost all military installations were concentrated in one area of the country.

Peter found that only the 1st Battalion was stationed in eastern Nigeria at Enugu. In western Nigeria, the 4th Battalion was at Ibadan, 2 Field Battery (Artillery) were at Abeokuta and 2 Reconnaissance Squadron were also at Abeokuta. The rest of the military establishment was in northern Nigeria.

The 3rd Battalion was at Kaduna, as were 1 Field Battery (Artillery), 1 Field Squadron (Engineers), 88 Transport Regiment, Nigeria Military Academy, Ordnance Depot, 44 Military Hospital, Nigeria Military Training College, Reconnaissance Squadron and Regimental Headquarters, Nigeria Air Force, 6th Battalion (under formation) and the ammunition factory. The 5th Battalion was at Kano; the recruit training depot and the Nigeria Military School were at Zaria. There were no military units in mid-western Nigeria and those in Lagos were either administrative or ceremonial. Both the 2 Field Battery and 2 Reconnaissance Squadron at Abeokuta in western Nigeria had moved there only recently because of the newly forged political alliance between the northern Nigeria leader, the Sardauna of Sokoto and Chief Akintola, then the western Nigerian parliamentary leader.

To some senior military officers of southern Nigerian origin, this concentration of military establishments in one part of Nigeria did not appear as a mere coincidence, and so they sounded a note of warning to some southern Nigerian politicians and leaders who were invariably un- interested. Thus in 1 964, the Quartermaster-General, a southern Nigerian, fought a one-man futile battle to prevent the establishment of the 6th Battalion in Kaduna and almost lost his job in the process.

With all major military installations in northern hands, the next phase of the operation to gain control of the army was to secure absolute majority within the rank and file of the army itself. Here the problems were formidable for the British government because, with the unlimited opportunities awaiting them in the field of politics and administration, the northerners showed little or no interest in the army. The ethnic quota system of recruitment into the army, which was introduced shortly before independence, provided the solution to the problem. Under this system, whenever new recruits were needed for the army, northern Nigeria would provide 60%, eastern and western Nigeria 15% each, and mid-western Nigeria 10%.

The north could hardly fill their quota and some southerners took advantage of the situation by passing for northerners and thus getting recruited into the army. In the name of "ethnic balance" military hospitals were staffed with "doctors" trained in Kano for about three years in preference to doctors of southern origin with internationally recognised diplomas.

The result of this system was that standards fell within the army – and soldiers became politically conscious. In order to ensure the loyalty of the military majority thus established, the criterion for promotion and advancement in the army was based more on political considerations than on efficiency or competence. Northerners would attain the rank of lieutenant-colonel and attend all available courses in military training colleges in Britain without even bothering to take the compulsory local "captain-to-major" promotion examination in Nigeria. At the same time, their southern Nigerian colleagues with them in the Royal Military Academy, Sandhurst were still captains.

This situation forced some southern officers who were politically conscious to identify themselves openly with political parties and politicians in order to gain military promotions and appointments without hindrance. Junior officers joined in the bitter struggle for military success through politics – a massive exercise which reduced the army and its promotions to a ridiculous farce. It could best be described as a football pool in which rich dividends were paid out to successful stakers.

For soldiers of northern Nigerian origin, the question of political alignment posed no problems for they were by birth aligned to the privileged establishment. Indeed, it was risky for a southern Nigerian commanding officer to punish a Northern soldier for fear of being accused of victimisation. The height of political manoeuvring among the military came when the commander of the 1st Brigade, a Yoruba brigadier from the south, closely identified himself with the party of northern Nigeria, the Northern People's Congress (NPC), in 1964, hoping by this move to command the Nigerian army on the departure of the last British general. In his eagerness to demonstrate his loyalty to the party, he consented to the request of the northern Nigerian premier, the Sardauna of Sokoto, for troops to be sent to the Tiv Division to quell political riots without clearance from the army headquarters in Lagos.

The commanding officer of the 5th Battalion based in Kano whose troops were to be sent, opposed the move, insisting on the need for proper procedure. The commanding officer was a southerner. He not only failed to stop the move but was immediately relieved of his command and posted to Lagos on the orders of the Sardauna.

The Yoruba brigadier, however, probably talked and boasted too much to the embarrassment of his political supporters and benefactors. When the time for the appointment eventually came, he did quite a lot of open campaigning to strengthen his position. Thus, with the help of the Sardauna, he fought and succeeded in having Ironsi, who had just returned from the Congo as a General with the United Nations forces, reverted to the rank of brigadier. Then using the northern government press and radio, he widely publicised his curriculum vitae and that of Ironsi, making sure that his own was the more impressive. The bulk of the southern army split into two opposing sides to campaign for the Yoruba brigadier and Ironsi, who showed little interest in the exercise. Ironsi was eventually appointed the GOC, but the struggle created a permanent division in the army.

Some officers, however, preferred to be neutral for, apparently, they considered a "*coup d'etat*" the only way of restoring the country's political and military situation to normality. These neutral officers, acting as umpires, saw no possibility of a return to normality by democratic means unless there was a change in the federal government.

In Nigeria, like most parts of Africa, where the policy is "once in power, always in power", only force could remove a government. It was not enough for the north to gain full control of the army; it also went a step further to use that army with abandon exclusively for the for the benefit of the Region.

For instance, the Reconnaissance squadron under a British major between 1958 and 1960 did nothing but carry out the wishes of the northern government. The Major who, as lieutenant-colonel, served in the British high commission in Lagos as the military attached during the Biafran civil war, was at that time a personal friend of the Sardauna, and therefore very influential among northern civil servants and politicians. In 1958, part of his unit conducted an operation throughout the northern region designed to exterminate the qualia birds that destroyed the grain. In 1959, this unit went to northern Cameroons (now Sardauna Province) to destroy lions alleged to be killing cattle in the Mambila plateau. Apart from those specific tasks, the army carried out "flag matches" all the year round in the northern region to reassure their leaders – privileges which were not extended to the south.

The involvement of the army in politics took a turn for the worst during the western Nigerian parliamentary elections in October 1965. The commanding officer of the 4th Battalion at Ibadan was alleged to have arranged for a training cadre on how to use military automatic weapons for Chief Akintola, the premier of western Nigeria, and his ministers. The premier was later killed in the January 1966 coup.

The malpractices that were alleged during the western regional elections were possible only because the army was said to have encouraged the dumping of ballot papers into the boxes in the polling booths by supporters of Akintola while they intimidated supporters of the opposing action group of Chief Awolowo. It had become clear that Nigeria was overdue for a change.

17

At midnight on 15 January 1966, a southern Nigerian major in Kaduna, the chief instructor of the Nigeria Military Training College, used a demonstration exercise which had been planned since October 1965 to stage what was hailed initially as a revolutionary coup.

His revolution aimed to get rid of the corrupt and incorrigible politicians and have them replaced with true nationalists. He said he regretted that it had become necessary to use force to do this when it could have been done through a democratic election – a system which was no longer possible in Nigeria. He eventually came unstuck because tribal and ethnic loyalties were much stronger than national and ideological loyalties.

It was striking that the major was conducting his coup almost entirely with soldiers of northern Nigerian origin. His medical attendants, driver, escorts and guards were all northern soldiers and he only ate meals prepared by his northern batman. Because of the major's intention to replace the old politicians with what he called "honest progressives" who would work under military supervision, he prepared a proforma to be signed by all politicians pledging their loyalty to the new regime and promising not to engage in any political or other activities likely to obstruct or retard the progress of the revolution.

All the politicians who were in Kaduna at the time of the coup signed this form before they left for their villages. Top civil servants were called into his brigade headquarters and, after pledging their loyalty, were briefed on their new duties under the new regime. The faces of the civil servants coming in and out of the headquarters portrayed nothing but joy cl d excitement.

The following day, 16 January, the major called a conference of all officers in Kaduna to brief them on what had been achieved and to issue instructions for future operations. Addressing the conference, he stressed his determination to deal ruthlessly with those who showed signs of "sitting on the fence" and the "opportunists".

Speaking about future operations he announced, 'I have grouped all forces under my control into three task forces. The first has been given the task of moving from the north to Zaria and Kano to consolidate our control on these areas and to remove all opposition where it still exists. The second task force has the assignment of moving through Jebba to take Ibadan (the western Nigerian capital) and subsequently Lagos. The third task force is to move on the eastern axis through Makurdi to take Enugu (the eastern Nigerian capital) and later Benin (the mid-western Nigerian capital). The task of the air force is to fit machine-guns to their Piagos and Donier training aircrafts in preparation for strafing and bombing Lagos when orders are given after the fall of Ibadan.'

The air force bombs were to be hand grenades and the pilots were already practising on the outskirts of Kaduna how to strafe with machine-guns and release grenades from their planes. Most, if not all of the officers attending this conference listened to the major's orders with absolute joy and manifest excitement. When the major in conclusion said, 'Nigeria has a population of fifty million. We can afford, and we are prepared, if need be, to sacrifice a million to achieve our aims and objectives,' the conference hall was virtually brought down by the applause of the young officers.

But things were not moving well for the revolutionaries in Lagos and southern Nigeria. At least they could be said to be partially successful with a task well planned but badly executed. Sir Abubakar Tafawa Balewa, the prime minister; Chief Okotie-Eboh, the federal minister of finance; Chief Akintola, premier of western Nigeria were all reported killed or missing. In the north, the Sardauna of Sokoto was reported killed in the early hours of the coup. However, it appeared that General Ironsi was successfully foiling the coup in southern Nigeria, thereby forcing the young officers there who started the coup in the south to flee into hiding in panic and fear.

Soon after this, what was left of the civilian regime quickly handed over full responsibility for the government of Nigeria to Ironsi. A stalemate was developing. The coup was completely over in the north with the major in command. Yakubu Gowon had come back from Britain on the night of 14 January 1966, a day before the coup started and had had narrow escapes from death in the hands of the revolutionaries. He soon became Ironsi's aide in his efforts to bring the major down to Lagos dead or alive.

The Major was well entrenched in the north but, through a senior southern officer intermediary, he conveyed a message to Ironsi that he was prepared to settle with Lagos under two main conditions:

'First and foremost is that the aims of the revolution shall be upheld at all times by the Lagos regime; secondly, I want guarantee of safety for myself and others who took part in the coup.'

Ironsi accepted the conditions and invited the major to Lagos. The major formally handed over power to Ironsi and agreed to go to Lagos. This enabled Ironsi to announce the appointment of military governors, one for each of the four regions: Ojukwu for the east; Ejoor for the mid-west; Lieutenant Colonel Francis Fajuyi for the west; and major Katsina for the north.

On 20 January 1966, in a short ceremony outside the brigade headquarters, the Major handed over the affairs of northern Nigeria to the newly appointed Governor, Katsina. Katsina made a short speech in praise and support of the major and all he stood and fought for. In the presence of the world press and radio, including the British Broadcasting Corporation (BBC), Katsina concluded, 'I am determined to ensure that the major's efforts will not be in vain.'

In a show of great emotion Katsina embraced the major before his final departure.

The January coup at the time was widely acclaimed all over the country, including the northern region, where the civil servants celebrated its success, and apparently happy ending, by holding parties both in their homes and in public places. People were drinking to the survival of a new Nigeria.

Western Nigeria probably benefited most from this revolutionary turn of events. The military takeover brought to an end a long nightmare of bloody riots which were triggered off by the rigged western Nigerian Parliamentary elections. In the east, west, mid-west and Lagos, the entire people and press hailed the change with absolute joy and optimism for the emergence of a new Nigeria free from corruption, tribalism and nepotism. Ethnic loyalties being what they were, it was later mischievously argued that eastern Nigerians were massacred in retaliation for their role in the January coup.

The January revolution was not a total failure for it secured its primary objective – the removal of the discredited civil regime.

"What went wrong", one highly placed senior military officer reflected, "was the inability of the coup to exploit its success".

When, therefore, the inevitable countercoup came on 29 July 1966, the Ironsi regime just wobbled and collapsed.

The plot to overthrow General Ironsi's government was slow, deliberate and systematic. Said to have been conceived in Ahmadu Bello University, Zaria, and worked out in detail by northern Nigerian civil servants and politicians, it was executed by the ruling northern civilians and their military counterparts.

Ironsi's regime, formed in the first instance on the basis of compromise between Ironsi and the major on the one hand, and Ironsi and the politicians on the other, aspired to rule successfully by compromise. For this reason, the regime tried to placate those who sought to destroy it and took no action on various substantiated reports available to it concerning plans to overthrow it.

A major conference of all emirs and chiefs of the north was held in Kaduna during the month of June 1966. At this meeting, the emirs and chiefs conveyed to Ironsi certain conditions which he had to meet if the north was to remain part of Nigeria. Chief among them was the abrogation of Decree No. 34 – the unification decree.

Before the conference, towards the end of May 1966 and in early June, very bloody and widespread riots against southerners had broken out in big northern cities like Kaduna, Kano, Jos, Zaria, Katsina and Sokoto. There was tremendous loss of life and property. The authorities, it seemed, largely turned a blind eye.

By the middle of July 1966, it was clear that the D-Day was fast approaching. Northern officers in western Nigeria and Lagos held conferences every Sunday afternoon in the Ikoyi residence of the recently promoted Colonel Murtala Muhammad. In addition, there was a daily gathering of those residing in Lagos in federal guards' barracks which was out of bounds to southerners.

Ironsi was not to be dispatched in the north during his forthcoming visit; Lagos was ruled out because all major units were commanded by Ibos; mid-western Nigeria would be most unsuitable because no troops were stationed there and sudden movement of troops towards that region would alert him.

It was now clear that western Nigeria was going to be the killing field, for it satisfied all the necessary requirements. The only battalion in western Nigeria was under the command of a northerner and the men on the planned exercises would be dealing with an indifferent population. Ironsi seemed determined to continue his goodwill mission tours of the country. When he came back from northern Nigeria, he left for mid-western Nigeria on 27 July 1966 and, as feared, never returned.

18

Peter's main preoccupation now was to get Elizabeth, Emma and Mark out of the country and back to Southampton. This he managed to do fairly easily through the help of friends in Lagos. It was a heart-rending and very distressing parting at Lagos airport, but Peter thought it was for the best in view of the deteriorating political situation.

Meanwhile, back at Kaduna Peter had met a wealthy Ibo trader, Emmanuel Uzomah, from his hometown of Owerri. He had sensed that there was worse to come. He had already sent his family home to eastern Nigeria and was now packing up his valuable belongings in his Mercedes Benz estate car and invited Peter to join him. This suited Peter perfectly. He almost made the fatal mistake of entering the car and consenting to an immediate departure. It dawned on him all of a sudden that the route ought to be checked first before the journey, even though his civilian friend considered this unnecessary and a waste of time.

At his insistence, Emmanuel hired a Volkswagen car and drove along the route for about thirty miles and reported back on locations and strengths of all military roadblocks. He knew the area and a few of the locals very well in the course of his business; he reported two major roadblocks between milestone three and seven from Kaduna. The last roadblock, he said, was manned by a strong contingent of artillery men; most of them were likely to know Peter. Emmanuel and Peter now realised the gravity of the situation and the amount of danger facing Peter.

Peter was confident he would be able to leave Kaduna making maximum use of his thorough knowledge of the town and surrounding villages. Before long he presented a simple plan which was carried out with success. The plan was for Emmanuel to take him in his hired Volkswagen car to Kaduna South.

'Before the first roadblock, we will turn left into a lane which leads for two miles into a new housing estate mostly occupied by expatriates,' Peter began to expound. 'At the end of this lane, the major roadblock can be seen 500 to 600 yards to the right. You must drop me off there, from where I will make my way on foot through the villages till I finally come out at milestone twelve along the road to Kafanchan. You should be at the rendezvous by 1400 hours to give me enough time to get there. You must use the Mercedes car to avoid any suspicion that could arise if the Volkswagen was used again, particularly as it has been thoroughly searched during your reconnaissance.'

By 1200 hours, Peter was ready to move, having changed into a big Hausa gown and cap donated by Emanuel. All he had on him was his revolver and 85 pounds worth of cash. By 1230 hours, Peter was already making his way through peaceful villages which were still completely unaware of what was happening in town. Peter spoke sufficient Hausa language to go through those villages without arousing curiosity or suspicion which proved a very useful asset.

Before 1400 hours, Peter was in the bush opposite the rendezvous. A big Mercedes was parked there facing Kaduna rather than Kafanchan. Peter crawled close to the car which was similar to Emmanuel's but he was not in a position to see the registration number. The car's bonnet was open, and the most disconcerting thing was that there was no sign of life anywhere near the car. Peter's mind raced through all sorts of possibilities. After lying there for 20 long minutes, he decided to make a move towards the car in the hope that he could shoot his way out of trouble if he encountered any.

With his revolver at the ready, he came out to the main road and looked around the car. It was indeed the right car but there was nobody around. Soon he heard some noise in a bush nearby. As Peter crawled into cover he heard a low deliberate whisper and Emmanuel emerged from behind the bush. He explained, 'The car had to face Kaduna so as not to give to passers-by who knew the situation the impression that someone was running away. Also, the idea of leaving the bonnet of the car open was to give the false impression that the car had broken down.'

'Good chap!' Peter congratulated him.

There was no time to be lost and very soon the car was speeding towards Kafanchan at a very brisk pace.

'Pray we don't run into another roadblock on our way,' Peter said, almost in a whisper.

'I'm not really the praying type, Peter, but I've learnt to sort of cross my heart and hope to survive in tight spots these days. Will that do?'

'Get on with you, you rascal!'

The nearer they were to Kafanchan the more relaxed they became. But suddenly a stray goat ran across their path as they were approaching a narrow bend and they were forced to pull up short. At the same time, a bus which seemed to have made a routine stop to allow passengers to relieve themselves was seen at the far end of the bend coming in the opposite direction. It was now gathering speed and tore around the bend, hitting the goat and killing it outright.

Emmanuel was sure the passengers were soldiers returning to Kaduna and gave the bus a wide berth almost to the point of keeling over the sharp serrated hard edge of the potholed road. He had seen them before in that bus and was not taking any chances. Neither was Peter, for he dived down quickly to the floor of the car in the back seat as the bus passed by. But he when he overheard snatches of the passengers' conversation he realised that they were mainly Ibo soldiers returning to Kaduna from leave, probably unaware of what was in store for them.

'Poor wretches,' Peter said to Emmanuel. 'I wish I could get out and warn them to turn back.' But he dared not.

As they were about to resume their drive to Kafanchan, Peter looked back and saw the bus carrying the soldiers almost disappear in the distance. Then they heard a sudden explosion and reports of rifle and machine-gun fire. The bus had been ambushed and set ablaze by northern soldiers who must have been keeping track of the bus's movements. Peter doubted if any of them escaped alive.

They sped on to Kafanchan without any further mishaps.

There they parted company.

'The best of luck, Peter,' said Emmanuel in a voice surprisingly choked with emotion, as he patted Peter on the back in a bear hug. 'I feel as if I've known you for ages. I think you'll make it. Well, I must look up my brother-in-law who lives inside Kafanchan itself. Look after yourself.'

'Thank you, Emmanuel, I will,' Peter replied swiftly. 'You must be as tough as an old army boot to have made your way in the world so successfully, considering you were orphaned when very young.'

'I shudder to think, Peter, how the new orphans of this crisis will fare. I was lucky in some ways being single-minded in my pursuits, though I think you do need lots of luck along the way to help you pull through. I got this pocket transistor radio for you to keep you company. I bet you'll probably hide in the bush for periods of time to avoid recognition. Here are some spare batteries. Again, look after yourself, and God bless, if I'm not being blasphemous!'

Peter was moved to tears but held himself in check. 'I mustn't lose control,' he said sharply to himself. He had to catch a train for Enugu as soon as possible. All trains were overcrowded, but Kafanchan seemed perfectly normal. All around, one could easily identify fleeing officers and men of southern Nigerian origin, despite their attempts at disguise. Inquiries at the station showed that the River Benue bridge at Makurdi had been sealed off by northern troops. All trains were thoroughly searched for eastern Nigeria officers, and those identified were said to have been shot on the spot and thrown into the river.

The troops stationed at Makurdi at the time were from the 5th Battalion Kano, under the command of a captain whom Peter knew would recognise him as would also most of his troops even if he wore a mask, for he had very recently been on a tour of duty to the units of the 5th Battalion in Kano. Having come so far he did not want to take a single risk and, though disappointed, he decided to hide in the bush and try again a few days later when things would hopefully have improved.

The radio stations heard on his pocket transistor radio carried little or nothing about the situation in Nigeria. Gowon had announced he had taken overpower and said something about the basis for unity in Nigeria not being there. Governor Ojukwu on his part had said something about not recognising Gowon; these statements added to rather than clarifying the confusion in Peter's mind. As days passed by, reports on the situation at Makurdi bridge showed gradual deterioration. By now, all train passengers had to get down on the bridge while searching and interrogation took up to eight hours for a passenger train. After four days in the bush Peter said to himself, 'I've had enough. I've just got to make a move now.'

There were many friendly southern civilians in the area who offered their homes as safe houses for fleeing southern officers. Some of the civilians were also beginning to pack up and move away towards Enugu. No civilians had yet been attacked in the area. Some of those leaving did so because they were warned or threatened by their northern neighbours. Others were simply afraid or panic-stricken.

The Ibo station master at Kafanchan said to Peter, 'I have arranged to move you down by train to a village ten miles from Makurdi. From there you should hire a bicycle for yourself and a local Ibo guide to take you to an obscure beach enclave from where you could cross by canoe.'

Peter rather liked and admired this balding, genial station master, Obed, who seemed to get on very well with all his staff whether of northern or of southern origin; he must have saved the lives of countless fleeing southerners. Peter thanked him for his efforts to arrange the train journey to the village.

While Peter was waiting in a safe house, he came to know four of his companions better. One was a sergeant-major chief clerk, the other an education instructor sergeant, both from the 3rd Battalion Kaduna. The third and fourth men, were private soldiers from the Military Hospital, Kaduna. The sergeant-major had bandaged hands. He narrated how his commanding official an Ibo lieutenant-colonel, was shot at midnight on 29 July 1966 in front of the battalion guardroom. He had been lured out there by his regimental sergeant-major who told him there was a very urgent matter requiring his presence. Having shot the commanding official an alarm for a battalion muster parade was sounded, the battalion yet unaware of the death.

On the parade ground, eastern Nigerians were extracted and loaded into waiting trucks. The trucks then drove to mile eighteen on the Kaduna-Jos road, and after the execution there of each group or truck load, the soldiers inspected the corpses using vehicle head lamps. When they were all certified dead, all valuables on the victims, particularly watches and rings, were removed. The sergeant-major said that he was not hit by a bullet but fell down with the dead and lay perfectly still during the inspection despite a terrible itch in his nostrils.

He was covered in the blood of others, and only lost his wristwatch during the inspection; as the lights went out and the executioners departed, the sergeant-major said he crawled away to safety and later made his way to Jos. He had injured both hands when he was pushed hard against the sharp metal edge of the truck that brought them to where they faced the firing squads. The Ibos in Jos gave him a change of clothes and some money and arranged for him to continue his journey to Enugu.

Then came the confession of the sergeant education instructor. 'I admit I was absent without leave on the fateful night.' He looked somewhat uncomfortable as he continued, 'I had spent the night at a woman-friend's house in town. The woman's husband almost caught me with my pants down, literally, and I had to make a hurried escape through the back window. I did not realise there was trouble during the night, how could I? However, on my way back to the barracks the following morning, I got to know what was happening. I just turned around and started making my way to eastern Nigeria.'

There was dead silence, then some polite coughs and chin-rubbing.

One of the two private soldiers felt encouraged to relate their own story.

'We were on duty on 29 July 1966 in the Kaduna Military Hospital. Just before 0100 hours the next morning, a military Land Rover stopped in front of the reception to the officers' ward. A few soldiers dismounted and ordered the duty sergeant to arrange to remove a 'parcel' in the vehicle which they had brought for the hospital. When a member of the staff went to collect the "parcel" it turned out to be the corpse of the Ibo lieutenant-colonel shot at midnight on 29 July in front of the battalion guard-room. As the hospital staff, who were nearly all eastern Nigerians, stood there speechless, one of the soldiers who brought the corpse in remarked in Hausa, *'"Ana yi ku, kwo ha ku gani ha?"* – "There is a coup going on, or don't you understand?"'

The private soldier paused, his fingers trembling a little. Then he concluded, 'At first we couldn't take it all in, but as soon as the Land Rover left, the staff took fright and scattered in all directions. '

Peter left the safe house and eventually got to the village ten miles from Makurdi in a goods train as arranged. He hired a bicycle and found a local Ibo guide at the third attempt. When he got near the beach enclave described, searchlights were sweeping the area. Peter laid low for a couple of hours. He dismissed the guide and paid him about fi pounds sterling.

'Thank you, sir,' the guide said deferentially. 'Thank you very much, sir. Safe journey.'

Five eastern Nigerian officers, including two lieutenant-colonels and a major, had crossed the Benue river by canoe from this beach enclave the previous night. The local fisherman who ferried them across told Peter that the northern soldiers at the bridge were becoming aware of these side-crossings and that after taking him across that would be it; though he was paid handsomely, it was becoming more dangerous by the hour. As they waited anxiously for the nightfall to darken, Peter's nerves were becoming very strained. The searchlights had not been turned on for more than an hour. The fisherman did not think they would be switched on in their direction for at least another hour. They made a dash for it to the opposite bank.

But in mid-stream, the searchlights suddenly swept their boat and a fusillade of rifle and machine-gun fire fatally wounded the fisherman who sank almost immediately with his boat as Peter was thrown into the river with a splash. The water was very cold and Peter stayed under as long as he could. He could feel the current swirl him and he stayed under until he thought he could never come up. The minute he did he took a breath and went down again. It was easy to stay under with so much clothing and his boots. When he surfaced the second time he saw a piece of timber ahead of him and reached it and held on with one hand. He kept his head behind it and did not even look over. There were more shots when he came up the first time but there were no shots later.

The piece of timber swung in the current and Peter held it with one hand. He looked at the bank. It seemed to be going by very fast. There was much wood in the river. The water was very cold. They passed the brush of an island above the water. He held on to the timber with both hands and let it take him along. The shore was out of sight now. Peter began to think how you do not know how long you are in a river when the current moves swiftly. It seems a long time and it may be very short. The water was cold and seemed in flood and many things passed that had been wafted off the banks when the river rose. Peter felt lucky to have a heavy timber to hold on to, and he lay in the cold water with his chin on the wood, holding as best he could with both hands. He was afraid of cramps and he hoped he would move toward the shore. They went down the river in a long curve. There was a brush island ahead and the current moved toward the shore. He wondered if he should take off his boots and clothes and try to swim to land but decided not to. He had never thought of anything but that he would reach the shore somehow, and he would be in a bad position if he landed barefoot. He had to get to Enugu some way.

He watched the shore come close, then swing away, then come closer again. The shore was very close now. The timber swung slowly so that the bank was behind him and he knew they were in an eddy. They went slowly around. As he saw the bank again, very close now, he tried holding with one arm and kicking and swimming the timber toward the bank with the other, but he did not bring it any closer. Peter was afraid they would move out of the eddy and, holding with one hand, he drew up his feet so they were against the side of the timber and shoved hard toward the bank. He could see the brush, but even with his momentum and swimming as hard as he could, the current was taking him away. He thought then he would drown because of his boots, but he thrashed and fought through the water, and when he looked up the bank was coming towards him, and he kept thrashing and swimming in a heavy-footed panic until he reached it.

Peter hung to a nearby branch of a tree and did not have strength to pull himself up but he knew he would not drown now. It had never occurred to him on the timber that he might drown. He felt hollow and sick in his stomach and chest from the effort, and he held to the branches and waited. When the sick feeling was gone he pulled into the bushes and rested again, his arms around some brush, holding tight with his hands to the branches. Then he crawled out and pushed on to the bank. He lay flat on the bank listening to the river with half an ear.

After a while Peter got up and started along the bank. He sat down by some bushes and took off his shoes and emptied them of water. He took off his coat, took his wallet with his papers and his money all wet in it out of the inside pocket and then wrung the coat out. He took off his trousers and wrung them too, then his shirt and underclothing. He slapped and rubbed himself and then dressed again. He had lost his transistor radio. His clothes felt wet and clammy and he slapped his arms to keep the circulation going. It was getting light and Peter started making his way to the Makurdi station which was on the other side of the notorious bridge which later became known as the Red Bridge of Makurdi because of the large number of southern soldiers that had been killed there. When he got there in the morning everybody on duty seemed to be of southern Nigeria origin, yet they went about their work happily and without fear. It was almost unbelievable that such a normal situation could exist in a railway station less than a mile from the Red Bridge where southern soldiers were being killed every hour of the day.

Later in the morning, Peter went across to the platform to catch a train for Enugu. He felt more relaxed having bought a change of civilian clothes and mingled freely with what was left of the good people of northern Nigeria. He resisted strong pressure from the Ibos who knew his story to stay and rest in Makurdi until evening. They meant well but thought that he was in a position to know that such a rest could be eternal. He also knew that their confidence that Makurdi would continue to be normal indefinitely was misguided and he told them so. He hoped his brief would make them sit up and plan their next moves with greater urgency and more realism.

19

The resumption of the killings brought with it an influx of refugees in eastern Nigeria from all over the federation of Nigeria. They came back by air, land and sea, in pathetic and shocking condition. Most had one or the other part of their bodies either broken or completely missing. Thousands of children arrived, some with severed limbs and many others emasculated. The adults bore the full brunt of the killings and very few arrived from the North unharmed. Women above the age of ten were raped and many of them came back on stretchers. Young women were gang-raped until some of them collapsed and died. Some pregnant women had un-mentionable things done to them and their unborn babies.

There was hardly a family in eastern Nigeria untouched by these terrible tragedies.

As could be expected, tempers were extremely high and volatile, particularly when those who managed to come back told their stories of cruelty and premeditated atrocities. The remaining eastern Nigerian soldiers in Lagos came back by air. They arrived either naked or in underpants, and the big gashes on their bodies showed they had been thoroughly beaten and tortured.

Offi from Lagos also told their own stories. The Ibo captain who was Ironsi's air force ADC and who was with Ironsi at the time of his death told the story in Enugu of how the general died.

'At 0630 hours on 29 July 1966, Ironsi, Fajuyi, the governor of western Nigeria and myself were arrested at Government House, Ibadan by northern troops under the command of captain Danj The troops used to carry out the arrests were the very ones detailed to protect the general during his tour. We were driven to an isolated jungle just outside Ibadan. By the time we got there, we had been so thoroughly beaten that the older two – Ironsi and Fajuyi – could hardly stand up. Shortly afterwards, Fajuyi was shot and then Ironsi, who remained tight-lipped and disdainful of his captors to the end.'

The captain paused, swallowed hard, his voice clotted with emotion, his eyes misting over with restrained tears, then continued.

'When Ironsi was shot, I ran into the bush and escaped. No, it wasn't as simple as that. My colleague, the northern Hausa ADC who was also present, wanted me to escape. During the month of June 1966, he and I had discussed the possibility of another coup. The northern Offi was emphatic the Ibos were going to do it again, but I swore it was going to be done by northerners. At the end of a long and heated argument, we came to an agreement that whichever side did it, the man on the winning side should save the others' lives. It was because of this agreement that the northern ADC whispered to me to escape while Ironsi was being shot whilst he distracted the attention of the soldiers.'

20

The news that Colonel Ojukwu was in Aburi, Ghana with the other military governors on 4 January 1967, to try to find a peaceful solution to the current disturbances in the country came as an encouraging surprise to many easterners. They suspended judgement on the atrocities they suffered in the north. At the end of the two-day conference, some important decisions were reached aimed at restoring the regions to their political position prior to the 15 January coup.

When Gowon returned to Lagos, he was apparently advised to reject the bulk of the decisions, particularly the re-convening of an ad hoe constitutional conference. Instead Gowon enacted Decree No. 8, which gave him power to declare a state of emergency in any region irrespective of the wishes of the Governor of that region. This was a clear indication that Gowon and his advisers were no longer giving much consideration the possibility of a peaceful solution. Rather they were now rapidly preparing the ground for the use of force.

A feeling of absolute helplessness seemed to have pushed the eastern Nigerian government to pass a couple of edicts to protect the interests of its people and avoid a total economic collapse of the region. These edicts were meant to serve as temporary relief while a more permanent solution was being sought. Foremost among these edicts were the Registration of Companies edict, the Revenue Collection edict, and the Court of Appeal edict. As an apparent punishment for these measures taken by the eastern Nigeria government, Lagos imposed sanctions on, and a blockade of, the eastern region.

As a result of the deteriorating situation, Colonel Ojukwu convened a meeting of the Advisory Committee of Chiefs and Elders at Enugu on 26 May 1967, to acquaint them with the latest development and seek their decision.

This was merely a continuation of the cherished mode of government in that part of Nigeria where consensus rule was an integral part of the ethnic culture. In the same vein, the pre-crisis premiers of eastern Nigeria, Dr Nnamdi Azikiwe (the first president of independent Nigeria) and Dr Michael Okwara, regularly consulted an ad hoe assembly of the Leaders of Thought and Opinion from the different provinces of the region to sound out grass-roots sentiments about the performance of their government, often leading to a significant adjustment of government policies. The Ibos, in particular, seem to have an innate aversion to autocratic rule and even their chiefs must rule by consent.

Colonel Ojukwu gave the Committee three alternative solutions to the crisis: to accept the terms of the north and Gowon and thereby submit to domination by the north; to continue the present stalemate, and drift; or to ensure the survival of the people by asserting their autonomy.

On 27 May, the Consultative Assembly mandated Ojukwu: 'To declare at the earliest practicable date Eastern Nigeria a free, sovereign, and independent State by the name and title of the Republic of BIAFRA. The Bight of Biafra formed the coastal border of the territory of the eastern region of Nigeria.

On 30 May, the formal declaration of the sovereign state of Biafra was announced by Ojukwu, the head of state.

21

Lagos's reaction to the declaration of the independent republic of Biafra was swift and immediate, for Gowon at once announced a pre-planned new constitution for Nigeria based upon the division of the existing four regions into twelve states. The eastern region was unilaterally split into three states, East Central, Rivers, and South-Eastern States, to undermine the ethnic dominance of the majority Ibos in the region.

The thought of being independent of Nigeria after what they had been through recently was understandably heady and glorious to the easterners, but to make this a reality was going to be a miracle; yet there was universal jubilation. Now, at least, they had a chance to have a say in what happened to their lives instead of being pushed around by an outfit that manifestly seemed to care little for other people's lives or property.

Militarily, however, there was some debate as to whether the date chosen for the declaration of independence was "the earliest practicable date". Almost all the senior Biafran army officers thought the answer to that question was an unqualified "No".

Peter's military intelligence reports estimated that what was left of the Nigerian army at Enugu barracks after the departure of the northerners amounted to about 240 soldiers, the majority of them technicians and tradesmen. As the weapons taken away by the northern soldiers were never returned, not all the remaining soldiers had weapons. This was what the nascent Biafran army was endowed with. Nigeria, on the other hand, had an army of six battalions, well-equipped by modern standards. In support were two artillery units holding a total of 16x105 mm pack howitzers in addition to two reconnaissance squadrons equipped with Ferret and Saladin armoured vehicles, not to mention mortars of various calibres. It had a sizeable navy and air force that could be made combat-ready at short notice.

****

As the threat from Lagos became more real, a conference of senior eastern army officers was held in Enugu. The conference recommended the formation of two new infantry battalions to be called the 7th and the 8th. These battalions were to be based at Nsukka and Port Harcourt, respectively. The daunting task of the 7th Battalion was to defend the entire northern Biafran border while the 8th Battalion defended the south, with the re-organised 1st Battalion acting as the army reserve force in addition to looking after the Niger river line western border of Biafra. On the morning of 6 July 1967 at 0530 hours at Garkem, about thirty miles from Ogoja town, close to the Biafran northern territorial boundary with Nigeria, some heavy rumblings were heard in two directions. The Nigerians were attacking in Garkem with two battalions advancing on two axes, right and left. Their preparatory bombardment using artillery and heavy mortars was extremely heavy and sustained.

The Biafran war had begun.

This first engagement seemed to have ended in stalemate. The Biafrans sensed from this encounter that they were not going to have much difficulty dealing with the Nigerian infantry. What remained to be sorted out, and very quickly too, was the problem posed by the Nigerian big guns, mortars and, especially, their armoured vehicles.

On the fourth day of the war, Nsukka, the university town on the Biafran northern border had fallen to the Nigerians.

By last light on 8 August 1967, Biafran troops sporting their Rising Sun uniform emblems, were secretly concentrated at Onitsha on the eastern bank of the River Niger, supported by the militia. After a couple of hours of unexplained delay, Colonel Banjo led the Biafran troops across the Niger bridge, Onitsha in the early hours of 9 August. Peter was with the leading motorised column in their lightning dash to Benin. It was heady stuff; morale was sky-high as they swept through miles and miles of Nigerian territory with scarcely any opposition. Early that morning Biafran troops captured Benin, the capital of mid-western Nigeria, with negligible loss of life. Within 48 hours, all the major towns in the whole region had been seized by the Biafrans in a three-pronged charge. A column of Biafran troops pressed on to Ore, threatening Ibadan, the capital of western Nigeria.

Formal recognition of Biafra as an independent sovereign state came from a small number of countries led by Tanzania

Ivory Coast and Gabon, perhaps on grounds of natural justice despite other pressures on them not to do so.

However, the Nigerians gradually reorganised, counter-attacked and rolled back the Biafrans across the River Niger by 8 October 1967, just as a long-suspected fifth column in the Biafran army was unmasked. The ring leaders, Colonel Banjo among them, were also accused of plotting a coup against the head of state. They were tried in Enugu and shot.

Following this, the morale of Biafran troops seemed to have suffered a crumpling body blow with no clear recovery till the end of the war. Most of the senior officers were no longer fully trusted by their men.

While Peter was making his way back to Biafra through the bush tracks near Ogwashiuku, he was suddenly confronted by an imposing black mercenary from the neighbouring Chad republic serving with the Nigerian troops. He lunged at Peter in a bayonet charge. Peter side-stepped, drew his pistol, and shot him fatally in the forehead. Papers in his breast pocket said he was a 35-year-old Chadian, and there was also a fading photograph of a very young woman in her teens, presumably his wife.

The next day Peter met up with a Biafran army major and explosives expert from Warri, making his way back to Onitsha. He told Peter how he had to intervene to stop the roughing up of some AGIP/ENI oilmen, mostly Italians, working in the riverine areas of mid-western Nigeria after they had been detained by Biafran militiamen for collaborating with the enemy, as the retreating Biafrans became more and more jittery and angry, sensing that militarily they were in pretty deep trouble.

22

By 29 September 1967 Enugu, the Biafran capital, had fallen to the Nigerians. Colonel Ojukwu had left Enugu on the 26th, 48 hours before the first Nigerian troops entered Enugu, to set up a new capital and administrative headquarters at Umuahia.

Peter was invited to join a select group of Biafran scientists and engineers on the research and production board called the Biafran Science Group. In their enthusiasm they considered no problem impossible to solve, given the means. They worked very hard to solve the problem of ammunition shortage by making available to the army a good quantity of their own products.

They designed and built several refineries and produced petrol and diesel at a considerable rate. Portable refineries for distilling crude oil in the field were commissioned. Biafran-made rifles, pistols, hand grenades, dry batteries, rockets, various species of mines like "ogbunigwes" were deployed. There were also non-military products like long- life foods and baby feeds.

On 19 November, Biafran troops re-entered and occupied Ogbete in Enugu, the town's main market, but their attempt to drive out the Nigerians and re-take the town was repulsed.

The Second Division of the Nigerian army under Colonel Murtala Muhammad entered Onitsha on 25 March 1968, after many months of intensive battles from Nsukka. The Biafrans then built solid defences around Onitsha in the hope that the Nigerian Second Division would be too tired to carry out any serious attacks for some time; they were largely right. But the loss of Onitsha was a military as well as an economic and social disaster for Biafra. On the tactical side, Nnewi, the hometown of Colonel Ojukwu, and the crucial Ibo heartland were now badly threatened. The Biafrans had also lost Onitsha Market, probably the largest in black Africa, and all that it contained. The market while it existed and functioned was the main source of supply to the army and the civilian population alike. With the added loss of the Onitsha textile mills, the army's clothing problem gravely worsened. Above all, the people of Onitsha now joined the refugee population, thereby increasing the already considerable refugee figures of the nation. With the later loss of Abakaliki went the greatest food producing area of Biafra. From then on, the threat of starvation in Biafra became more real.

Most of southern Biafra, with non-Ibo ethnic majority groups, fell more easily to the Nigerians. Ikot-Ekpene fell on 12 April 1968, though it was later recaptured by Biafran troops only to be retaken by the Nigerians not long afterwards. To the Biafrans the loss of Port Harcourt on 24 May was one of the biggest setbacks of the war. Apart from the adverse effects it might have politically on the Kampala peace talks, it was a military as well as an administrative disaster for Biafra. Because of the loss, both the Biafran air force and navy ceased to be operational for quite some time.

The science group lost the bulk of their stores and equipment so vital for the manufacture of their war products which had kept the army going. The Biafrans had lost the Port Harcourt oil refinery and most of the oil wells, not to mention the big department stores. There was to be no more electricity in Biafra with the loss of the Afam gas supplies. Even the ammunition to continue the war would not come in for several days until Uli airport was commissioned.

A seething mass of Biafran refugees left Port Harcourt for the Ibo heartland with what possessions they could carry with them.

Not long afterwards, the rapid loss of Aba, Owerri, and Okigwe nearly broke the will of the Biafran people to continue the war. The social problems, particularly with respect to refugees, were much more than the country could handle adequately. The food problem was now very acute. On 6 January 1969, the Biafran army started an operation to lay siege to Owerri and recapture it and were within a mile of the town centre when news broke on 27 March that the First Division Nigeria army had started a very major offensive to capture Umuahia, the new Biafran capital, calling in massive air support that bombarded the town over and over again. The final push to seize Owerri was stalled. On 18 April when it seemed obvious Umuahia was going to be lost, the Owerri operations were resumed.

The Nigerians fi entered Umuahia town on 22 April 1969. Many Biafrans regarded the loss of Umuahia as a logical end of the war. But three days later, Biafran troops recaptured Owerri after encircling the entire Nigerian brigade bottled up in the town centre.

The skilful and timely execution of the Owerri siege and victory revived the dying Biafra. All Biafrans who, a few days before, wanted nothing but an end to the war now pressed for the continuation of the struggle to the end. Owerri quickly became the new Biafran capital. The Biafran head of state, now General Ojukwu, put out a long list of promotions to commemorate the recapture of Owerri.

In May 1969, General Ojukwu set up a joint planning committee chaired by himself, with the Chief of Staff, General Philip Efi (a non-Ibo from south-eastern Biafra), and the commanders of army, navy, and air force as members. This was designed to satisfy civilian and military pressures, which had existed since the beginning of the war, in favour of the establishment of a war council. It was also hoped by this move to regain the confidence of the Biafran people and lessen the chances of the scourge of "saboteurs" ever again taking a stranglehold on the nation's war effort.

The Joint Planning Committee met once a week from May 1969 to the end of the war, but lack of resources meant that scarcely any of its operational plans were carried out.

23

Just before the dramatic collapse of Biafra in January 1970, in the wake of widespread malnutrition and food and other shortages, Peter got a letter via the International Committee of the Red Cross (ICRC) that his wife and two children had been fatally injured in a multiple motorway pile-up in thick fog near Reading.

The week before he had dreamed about them. He couldn't quite remember the mixed-up details of the dream except that he was back with his family and somehow Mark and Emma let go of his hands when they were walking a tight-rope across a ravine. The children sailed to safety on wings like birds to the other side of the ravine, leaving Peter struggling to regain his balance on the tight rope. Then he awoke in a cold sweat but was relieved it was just a dream. Peter sat unmoving on his chair. He sat quiet as if he had taken a dose of opium. The violence of the emotions he had passed through produced a feeling of exhausted serenity. He had plumbed in minutes the depths of horror and despair, and now found repose in the conviction that life had things up its sleeve you often can't do anything about circumvent.

When darkness fell, he listened to the night outside and, slowly, the hopelessness which he had known must come, engulfed him. He lay down and turned his face into the darkness of the pillows; but his eyes were alive with light. He sat up again, shuddering.

He heard a boom of thunder, and saw, as he had done many times, the lightning flicker on his shadowed wall. Now it seemed as if the night were closing in on him, and his room was bending over like a candle, melting in the heat. He heard the crack, crack; the restless moving of something above, and it seemed to him that a vast haunting body, like a human spider, was crawling over the roof, trying to get inside. He felt alone and defenceless. He was shut in a small black box, the walls closing in on him, the roof pressing down. He was in a trap, cornered and helpless. Gradually, hardly moving, he let his legs down over the dark edge of the bed. He paused. A movement of lightning on the walls forced his legs back on the bed. Nothing could be seen until the lightning plunged again, when the crowding shoulders of the trees outside showed against a cloud-packed sky. The lightning ran and danced, illuminating stormy ranges of cloud. All Peter's senses were stretched and he breathed rigidly in little gasps. Again, he heard the thunder growl and shake in the trees, lighting up the sky. It was beginning to rain and big drops blew across the windowpanes with a watery glimmer. Then the dark and his hopelessness returned.

Next morning, he stood up. Another day had come. His heart thumped and he felt hot all over. But his mind was made up. He was getting away from it all to make a new life for himself. At the start of the war, he had been on an intelligence mission down the eastern frontier of Biafra joining the Cameroons. He knew exactly where he wanted to go – a legendary secluded village called Gonzo. He just wanted to breathe again, freely.

When Peter arrived at Gonzo, a heavy mist had descended upon the village: the mist penetrating, enveloping, and silent; the morning mist of tropical lands. When the mist lifted, Peter gazed down on the green valley of Gonzo from the top of the little hills that surrounded it. He said to himself, 'Now if there could be a sign, it would be perfect. I know this is the place, but if only there could be an omen…

He looked into the sky, but it was clear of both birds and clouds. Then the breeze that blew over the hills in the evening sprang up. The palm trees made furtive little gestures toward the valley, and on the hillside a tiny whirlwind picked up a few leaves and flung them forward. Peter chuckled. 'My answer! Can't have a broader hint from the gods than that.'

He unrolled his blankets and laid them on the grass of the hillside. He lay on this and gazed down on the valley which was to be his home. On the far side, near a grove of fi palm trees, was the place; behind the chosen spot there was a hill, a little brushy crease, a stream, surely.

24

As the day drew in, the light became uncertain and magical. Peter sighed with contentment and lay on his back. The sky was prickling with stars. He saw a beautiful young woman getting dressed after a swim in a somewhat shady and concealed part of the stream.

Peter's breathing choked. She had a most stunning figure and a mass of raven hair. Her movements were delicate but precise. As she leaned over to dry her feet with a towel, Peter struggled vainly to take his eyes off her very thin dress and her uncluttered shape sharply defi beneath it, her well-formed and fi breasts that strained sensually against the delicately moist and clinging dress. She threw a light "lappa" cloth over herself, picked up a basket-load of papaws and disappeared in the grove of palm trees. Peter found himself trailing her.

In his bachelor days, Peter had not been able to look at any girl without idly considering marriage; and thoughts of marriage often produced more serious ones of it going wrong. This had made him shy with women to begin with. Marriage was a risk. A married couple that did not get on could be an awful thing, with two heads and eight limbs, a monstrous octopus, really, with a huge appetite and a short life. He feared this lonely captivity in marriage, this joyless solitude that would arrest him in his dreamed adventure, deprive him of true companionship, he and his partner seeming like a couple of deviants.

But with Elizabeth he felt he had been lucky. She was gay and vivacious and kind. He now and again consoled himself with his own private candid shots of her when they were newly married… the fi time she stood before him stark naked, making unusual gestures, cupping a breast lightly in one hand and with the deft fingertips of the other stroking her nipple, watching it harden…

During his marriage Peter had been able to look at any girl without worrying about marrying her. He stopped staring up the skirts of seated women or down their blouses in a bus queue; he could watch their shadowed parts, package-firm in tight clothes, and be tempted by no mystery or little challenge. It made him calm and gave him poise. And so, it came as quite a shock to Peter, after arriving in Gonzo and seeing that young woman, to feel the primeval urge waking in him. But he restrained himself.

As he ventured down the valley, his spirits rose. The valley he felt had in it all that the heart of man could desire – sweet water, pasture, even climate, slopes of rich brown soil with tangles of shrubs that bore excellent fruit; great hanging forests of palm, iroko, baobab, and mahogany trees. In this valley it seemed it neither rained nor sunned overmuch and the abundant springs gave a rich green pasture, irrigation spreading over all the valley space.

It also seemed the inhabitants did well indeed here. Their beasts looked well with shiny coats and were plentiful. But it did not take Peter long to discover that one thing marred their happiness. A strange disease had come upon them and had made all the children born to them there – and, indeed, several older children also – severely deaf. And amidst the little population of this now isolated and apparently forgotten valley the disease ran its course.

The old retained a sort of hearing, the young heard but very little, and the children that were born to them never heard at all initially. But life was very easy in that basin, the young women and girls most comely and uninhibited. With no evil insects nor any savage beasts. They were of simple stock. Generation followed generation. They forgot many things; they devised many things. In all things save hearing they were strong and able.

When at last Peter came through the grove of palm trees he was met by four men who stood side by side, looking him straight in the eye, judging him by his unfamiliar demeanour. There was an expression near puzzlement on their faces.

'This man,' one said in hardly recognisable pidgin English, 'must be another spirit coming down from the hills.'

But Peter advanced with the confident steps of a youth who enters upon life. And very civilly he gave them greeting. He talked to them in pidgin English, supplemented by sign language.

'Where does he come from?' asked another. 'Down out of the hills. '

The cloth of their coats Peter saw was curiously fashioned, each with a different sort of stitching.

'Come hither,' said yet another, grasping him firmly.

And they held Peter and examined him minutely, saying no word further until they had finished.

'Carefully!' Peter cried.

They scarcely seemed to heed him. 'Carefully,' he said again.

'This is a marvellous occasion,' the eldest among them said. 'Certainly, he is a man and has two balls down there. Let us lead him to the elders. '

Just then one of them farted rather noisily. Peter tried his utmost not to laugh but it was no use. He burst into a paroxysm of cathartic laughter.

'As you will,' said Peter, and was led along laughing.

He saw a number of figures gathering together in the middle roadway of the village. He found it taxed his nerve and patience more than he had anticipated, this first encounter with the population of Gonzo. He wished for a glass or two of beer to wash over his strained nerves.

The place seemed large as he drew near to it, the dwellings stranger, and a crowd of children and men and women – the women and girls he noted were very shapely indeed, touchingly doe-eyed – came about him, holding on to him, touching him with soft sensitive hands, smelling at him and listening hard at every word he spoke.

Some of the maidens and children, however, kept aloof as if afraid, and indeed his voice seemed coarse and rude beside their softer notes. They mobbed him. His four captors kept close to him and said again and again, 'A strange man out of the hills. '

'I am Peter.'

'A strange man – using strange words,' said one of his captors. 'Did you hear that – PATWA? He has only the beginnings of speech.'

A little boy pinched his hand. 'PATWA!' he said mockingly.

'Bring him to the elders,' they said once again.

They led him through a doorway into a room, at the end of which there faintly glowed a fire. For a moment, he struggled against a number of hands that clutched him. It was a one-sided fi There was a pause as if the people about him were trying to understand his words.

Then the voice of the chief of the elders began to question him. The interview and audience seemed to last for ages. Afterwards one of the maidens brought him food and led him into a lonely hut to eat out of their hearing and to slumber till the morning.

But Peter slumbered not at all. Instead, he sat up in the place where they had left him, resting his limbs and turning the unanticipated circumstances of his arrival at Gonzo over and over in his mind. Every now and then he laughed, sometimes with amusement, and sometimes with indignation. He was still thinking when the sun rose.

Peter had an eye for all beautiful things. His eyes went from the inaccessible glory of the splendid sunrise to the village and irrigated fields, resplendent in the technicolour sunburst. Suddenly, a wave of emotion took him, and he thanked God from the bottom of his heart for being alive. He heard a voice calling to him from out of the village.

'Ya ho there, Patwa! Come hither!'

At that Peter stood up smiling. 'Here I am,' he said.

'Have some good news for you,' the voice continued.

Peter was informed the chief of the elders personally approved of him and he was going to be granted the citizenship of Gonzo – but after he had learned the manner and customs of the place.

They led a simple, laborious life, these people, with all the elements of virtue and happiness, as these things can be understood by men. They toiled, but not oppressively; they had food and clothing sufficient for their needs; they had days and seasons of rest and jollification; they made much of music and singing; and there was passion and love-making among them, and little children.

One of the first customs that Peter became aware of was that of "age-mates". As far as the girls were concerned, it meant doing things together and alike, such as performing their outing dance. They also swam together in secluded parts of a stream, naked except for heavy beads around their waists which barely covered their secret parts.

Next came the custom of "open play" in which boys came into the girl's mother's hut for what they referred to as night games. As one of the maidens amplified, 'Boys would come into your mother's hut and play at fondling your breasts and licking your nipples with the tip of their tongue. You are supposed to try as much as possible to ward them off and not be bad-tempered about it. So long as you do not let him go too far and it is done inside the hut where an adult is near, it is alright.'

Some girls did eventually marry their early sweethearts, but in most cases the boys were either too young to afford bride price or were not ready for marriage. They not infrequently stood by and watched their fi loves married off to men often old enough to be their fathers.

However, it was regarded as shameful for a man no longer to be able to satisfy his wife sexually; rather than admit it, he would go out of his way to pay the bride prices of many more, in order to enhance his masculine image. An impotent man was very rare in the village! The few that existed were no more than living dead.

25

After the initial excitement had worn off, Peter found it rather lonely in the evening sitting on the veranda of his hut drinking the local brew by himself. It was the nights that did for him. He felt all alone. Over in the village centre he heard the sound of a gong or firecrackers. They were having a good time; they weren't so far away, but he stayed where he was. When his spirits were really low he felt he couldn't have been more of a prisoner if he'd been in jail. Night after night it was the same. He tried going to bed immediately after his evening meal but he couldn't sleep.

He used to lie in bed, wider awake, till he didn't know what to do with himself. Those nights were long.

Then one day, after his evening meal, he heard someone give a little cough. It was one of his original captors, Juba, the strongman of the village. He said, 'Aren't you lonely in that hut all night by yourself?'

'Oh, no, that's alright,' Peter said. He did not want Juba to know what a damned fool he was, but he expected Juba knew alright.

He stood there without speaking and Peter knew he wanted to say something to him.

'What is it?' Peter said. 'Spit it out.'

Then Juba said, 'If you'd like to have a girl to come and live with you I know who is willing. She is a very good girl and I can recommend her. She'd be no trouble and it would be someone to have about the place. She'd mend your things for you...'

Peter was feeling pretty low. He knew he wouldn't sleep once again for hours.

'You look,' Juba said, 'if you don't like her, away she goes.'

'Where is she?'

'She's here,' Juba said, 'I'll call her.'

Juba went to the door. The girl had been waiting close by. She came in and sat down on the floor. She was shy, of course, but cool enough, and when Peter said something to her she gave him a smile. She was probably in her late teens and awfully pretty. Her name was Leelah. They began to talk. She didn't say much, but she laughed a lot when Peter chaffed her.

Juba said, 'You'll fi she has plenty to say for herself when she gets to know you.'

'Come and sit by me,' Peter entreated.

She giggled and refused. She blushed and laughed but eventually came and sat on the chair beside Peter, snuggling up to him.

Juba laughed too. 'You see, she's taken to you already,' he said. 'Do you want her to stay?'

'Do you want to, Leelah?' Peter said to her.

She hid her face, laughing, on Peter's shoulder. She was very soft and warm.

'Very well,' Peter said, 'let her stay.'

That night, Leelah showed Peter how to make love the way he never dreamed of. She stood barring the doorway to his bedroom toying with the bead strings that formed a sort of curtain. There was a feeble light from the lantern behind her and it shone through her very, very thin and skimpy white cotton night shirt, sharply defi her womanly parts and curves. One hand was on her hip, which was slung sideways in a pose of daring sauciness, and her feet were apart.

Peter looked here and there and then at Leelah who smiled lusciously.

'You like?' she whispered.

In the morning when Peter woke, Leelah snored contentedly beside him, curled up, sleeping with her arms folded against her breasts, legs poised like a cyclist's. Peter shifted himself to a sitting position. The girl groaned, stopped snoring, but did not wake. Peter swung his legs over the side of the bed and looked for his trousers. When he stood and stretched, the girl woke up. She looked sleepily at him, then shook her head and sighed languidly. She suddenly pulled him down to the bed, giggling shyly, as she drew a sheet across her nakedness. Peter extricated himself by tickling her after she had lingeringly tattooed him with kisses and bites.

In next to no time, Peter's mood had undergone a sea change. His new life was now positively charmed and blissful, his past life just a faint memory.

And so, Peter became a citizen of Gonzo, and the people ceased to be people generally and became individuals and familiar to him, while the world beyond the hills became more and more unreal. He sought opportunities of doing Leelah and other citizens little services. When he was ill for some days, Leelah nursed him tenderly and that refined his sense of belonging.

After rallying, Peter proposed marriage to Leelah. 'You don't have to,' she protested.

'I do want to, very much, Leelah,' Peter insisted.

It was a simple ceremony witnessed by the elders and the great doctor among the people of Gonzo, their medicine man. He drew blood from the flesh of the couple's left ring fingers; they pressed the wounds together till their bloods mixed and sealed their bleeding as a token of their union. Earlier Leelah had resolutely refused payment of any bride price on her behalf – otherwise she would run away.

But Peter gave her family substantial presents in cloths and trinkets.

26

For some reason, the weather in Gonzo became more erratic and less predictable. Tonight, it was raining. Peter stood at their veranda, mutely watching the empty street awash in the rain. It had been raining most of the day, steady drizzle in the morning, beating wind in the afternoon, and now a straight heavy shower which poured ceaselessly out of the cold night.

The somewhat dry season had been wet, and so the wet season was uncertain. For days, the sun would shine, and then came the reminder that it was late November. At other times, this rain gave life; now the rain swelled rivers and washed-out bridges, turned dust into muck, and saturated crumbling turf, making it slick; it inconvenienced and killed. The people of Gonzo had never seen anything like this for a long, long time, They wondered what the gods would throw at them next.

At the street's edge, an open drain frothed full of rotten water and flotsam. A black cat, fl on its back, paws aloft, shot past, rigid in death. This was followed by a dead snake; it seemed strange and portentous. A black cat crossing your path over here did not signify, but a snake doing so was ominous.

A lightning bolt rent the sky, three-pronged. The street blistered with big raindrops. Around nine there was a particularly intense flash of lightning. It illuminated the whole place. Then just as quickly in the whoosh of sudden darkness, there was an ear-splitting crack of thunder. In the bedroom Leelah sat bolt upright and listened to that last thunderclap fading, a thudding rumble, like a big piano being shoved on wooden castors.

The morning after the storm, Gonzo was cool and had a sweet breath; it sparkled, the sun was gigantic in a cloudless sky, brown kites and pied ravens swooped on the storm's leavings, and other birds soared so high they appeared motionless. All the dusty trees of the village had been renewed by the rain, the leaves washed green, the withered blossoms knocked off. The fresh branches still dripped.

27

Over the past few days Leelah was quiet, cat-like, purring beside Peter who felt the fast thump of her heart and was deliciously conscious of the full boneless dumpling of her breast pressed against him. She would not leave Peter's side.

And at night, with feline wonder she was hyperattentive to Peter's passion and antics, showing her even sparkling teeth as she helped his groping hand which was like a blind man lightly translating her body's braille. Peter was struck anew by how pretty she was, and though he had not married her for that, he would have settled for the company of her simple presence, it was welcome.

He did not pretend to know much about her – he scarcely knew her at all he often thought – but her loveliness was unhidden. Of this Peter was positive. It bordered on error; it was so generous. She was firm – and slim. She had a long, graceful neck and large melting eyes; she was not black but brown. From the waist up, she was gently moulded, like the handle of a dagger; her breasts were like ripe mangoes, fi and uplifted. Her legs were shapely and her ankles well turned. But her ears were slightly larger than most women's ears, or perhaps seemed so when not hidden by hair.

The following week, Leelah whispered playfully in Peter's ear, as her vernacular put it, that she "had something on her person". Peter was not quite sure what she meant.

A month later, there was a distinct swelling in Leelah's stomach, the half-globe of a heavy meal. It stayed. It grew. Now there was no doubt.

Peter was very thrilled and treated Leelah almost like an invalid. His great fear was that something would go wrong with the bearing of the child. Peter would sit beside her and stroke her hand soothingly. Leelah liked to have him stroke the palm of her hand, firmly enough so it did not tickle. He talked to her quietly. She would squeeze his hand in gratitude and wanted more than ever before to make him happy. The birth was a very severe one. When it was over, and Leelah lay pale and exhausted in bed, Peter brought their little son and put him beside her.

The next day, POM. POM. POM. The village gong man went around Gonzo with unwelcome news. There was a kind of death coming from over the hills. The rumours that had been going around were indeed true. Several people had already died and the death toll was mounting. They called it *felenza* – influenza – a white man's death. The elders, after consultations, decided that the whole village should be warned.

Everybody felt a kind of chill and body aches. This *felenza* was something the white man had shot into the air, though everyone wondered why. Or perhaps, as the soothsayer suggested, punishment from the gods. Some of the elders remembered something like it about five or more years back, soon after a white missionary intruder was chased off Gonzo with an arrow in his back.

Within days men started dropping down dead on their farms. Death was always so sudden that the relatives and friends were too shocked to cry. The strong man of Gonzo, Juba, was one of the fi to go under. Leelah and her baby son were quickly carried off by the illness. Peter himself was in delirium for days with severe splitting headaches. When he came to and realised what had happened to Leelah and their baby son, he shot himself in the right temple with his Biafran pistol.

A month later, the *felenza* crisis was over.

****

CPSIA information can be obtained
at www.ICGtesting.com
Printed in the USA
LVHW050318140222
711073LV00009B/467